Stay away . . .

The girls were sitting in a circle around the Ouija board in the Wakefields' dimly lit living room.

Jessica's fingers rested lightly on the marker that was placed in the middle of the board. Letters from the alphabet ran along the perimeter of the board on two sides.

"What are we supposed to do besides sit here?" Lila whispered. "I mean, staring at this marker is getting kind of boring."

"Shhh," Ellen hushed her. "We have to wait for the spirits of Sleepy Hollow Road to send their message."

Suddenly, the marker began to shake and vibrate. Then it shot toward the S.

"It's working," Kala said with a gasp.

"Shhhh," Janet warned.

The marker slid toward the T.

"S T," Mandy whispered. "It's spelling something."

The marker began to dart crazily around the board, furiously spelling out words.

"'Stay'!" Mandy cried. "It spelled 'stay.'"

The marker skidded over to the A. And then in rapid succession it slid to W, back to A, and then to Y.

The girls looked at one another in silence.

"'Stay away'?" Mary said quietly.

Bantam Books in the SWEET VALLEY TWINS AND FRIENDS series.
Ask your bookseller for the books you have missed.

#1	BEST FRIENDS	#42	JESSICA'S SECRET
#2	TEACHER'S PET	#43	ELIZABETH'S FIRST KISS
#3	THE HAUNTED HOUSE	#44	AMY MOVES IN
#4	CHOOSING SIDES	#45	LUCY TAKES THE REINS
#5	SNEAKING OUT	#46	MADEMOISELLE JESSICA
#6	THE NEW GIRL	#47	JESSICA'S NEW LOOK
#7	THREE'S A CROWD	#48	MANDY MILLER FIGHTS BACK
#8	FIRST PLACE	#49	THE TWINS' LITTLE SISTER
#9	AGAINST THE RULES	#50	JESSICA AND THE SECRET STAR
#10	ONE OF THE GANG	#51	ELIZABETH THE IMPOSSIBLE
#11	BURIED TREASURE	#52	BOOSTER BOYCOTT
#12	KEEPING SECRETS	#53	THE SLIME THAT ATE SWEET VALLEY
#13	STRETCHING THE TRUTH	#54	THE BIG PARTY WEEKEND
#14	TUG OF WAR	#55	BROOKE AND HER ROCK-STAR MOM
#15	THE OLDER BOY	#56	THE WAKEFIELDS STRIKE IT RICH
#16	SECOND BEST	#57	BIG BROTHER'S IN LOVE!
#17	BOYS AGAINST GIRLS	#58	ELIZABETH AND THE ORPHANS
#18	CENTER OF ATTENTION	#59	BARNYARD BATTLE
#19	THE BULLY	#60	CIAO, SWEET VALLEY!
#20	PLAYING HOOKY	#61	JESSICA THE NERD
#21	LEFT BEHIND	#62	SARAH'S DAD AND SOPHIA'S MOM
#22	OUT OF PLACE	#63	POOR LILA!
#23	CLAIM TO FAME	#64	THE CHARM SCHOOL MYSTERY
#24	JUMPING TO CONCLUSIONS	#65	PATTY'S LAST DANCE
#25	STANDING OUT	#66	THE GREAT BOYFRIEND SWITCH
#26	TAKING CHARGE	#67	JESSICA THE THIEF
#27	TEAMWORK	#68	THE MIDDLE SCHOOL GETS MARRIED
#28	APRIL FOOL!	#69	WON'T SOMEONE HELP ANNA?
#29	JESSICA AND THE BRAT ATTACK	#70	PSYCHIC SISTERS
#30	PRINCESS ELIZABETH	#71	JESSICA SAVES THE TREES
#31	JESSICA'S BAD IDEA	#72	THE LOVE POTION
#32	JESSICA ON STAGE	#73	LILA'S MUSIC VIDEO
#33	ELIZABETH'S NEW HERO	#74	ELIZABETH THE HERO
#34	JESSICA, THE ROCK STAR	#75	JESSICA AND THE EARTHQUAKE
#35	AMY'S PEN PAL	#76	YOURS FOR A DAY
#36	MARY IS MISSING	#77	TODD RUNS AWAY
#37	THE WAR BETWEEN THE TWINS	#78	STEVEN THE ZOMBIE
#38	LOIS STRIKES BACK	#79	JESSICA'S BLIND DATE
#39	JESSICA AND THE MONEY MIX-UP	#80	THE GOSSIP WAR
#40	DANNY MEANS TROUBLE	#81	ROBBERY AT THE MALL
#41	THE TWINS GET CAUGHT	#82	STEVEN'S ENEMY

Sweet Valley Twins and Friends Super Editions

#1	THE CLASS TRIP	#3	THE BIG CAMP SECRET
#2	HOLIDAY MISCHIEF	#4	THE UNICORNS GO HAWAIIAN

Sweet Valley Twins and Friends Super Chiller Editions

#1	THE CHRISTMAS GHOST	#5	THE CURSE OF THE RUBY NECKLACE
#2	THE GHOST IN THE GRAVEYARD	#6	THE CURSE OF THE GOLDEN HEART
#3	THE CARNIVAL GHOST	#7	THE HAUNTED BURIAL GROUND
#4	THE GHOST IN THE BELL TOWER		

Sweet Valley Twins and Friends Magna Editions

THE MAGIC CHRISTMAS   A CHRISTMAS WITHOUT ELIZABETH

SWEET VALLEY TWINS
AND FRIENDS
SUPER CHILLER

The Haunted
Burial
Ground

Written by
Jamie Suzanne

Created by
FRANCINE PASCAL

BANTAM BOOKS
NEW YORK • TORONTO • LONDON • SYDNEY • AUCKLAND

RL 4, 008-012

THE HAUNTED BURIAL GROUND
A Bantam Book / October 1994

*Sweet Valley High® and Sweet Valley Twins and Friends® are
registered trademarks of Francine Pascal*

Conceived by Francine Pascal

*Produced by Daniel Weiss Associates, Inc.
33 West 17th Street
New York, NY 10011*

Cover art by James Mathewuse

ISBN: 0-553-56404-8

Published simultaneously in the United States and Canada

*Bantam Books are published by Bantam Books, a division of Bantam
Doubleday Dell Publishing Group, Inc. Its trademark, consisting of the
words "Bantam Books" and the portrayal of a rooster, is Registered in
U.S. Patent and Trademark Office and in other countries. Marca
Registrada. Bantam Books, 1540 Broadway, New York, New York 10036.*

PRINTED IN THE UNITED STATES OF AMERICA

OPM   0 9 8 7 6 5 4 3 2 1

To John Stewart Carmen

One

◇

Creak, creak.

There it was again.

As she rode her bicycle home from her friend Lila Fowler's house, Jessica Wakefield kept hearing that awful creaking noise.

Her bike wobbled slightly as she looked over her shoulder for about the fifteenth time. But all she saw behind her was a long stretch of dark, deserted pavement. On either side of her, the streetlamps glowed through the damp fog, casting a dim and eerie light.

She was beginning to wish that she had listened to her mother. They had spoken over the phone about half an hour before Jessica left the Fowlers' mansion.

"It's pretty dark out," her mother had said.

"Don't you want me to come pick you up?"

Jessica had rolled her eyes at Lila. "I'll be fine," she had told her mother irritably. "It's only a few blocks."

"Do you want me to send Steven over to ride home with you?" her mother had persisted.

Jessica had heard her older brother Steven's squawk of protest and her mother's muffled retort in the background.

Steven Wakefield was fourteen and a freshman at Sweet Valley High School. Jessica and her twin sister, Elizabeth, were in sixth grade at Sweet Valley Middle School. The twins were twelve years old, but sometimes it seemed to Jessica that her mother treated them as though they were ten.

Tonight, for instance. Mrs. Wakefield had made such a big deal about Jessica getting home, even though Jessica had ridden her bike home from Lila's a million times. But just because it was dark and a little rainy, her mother had acted as if Jessica were embarking on some dangerous journey.

Talking on the phone with her mother, Jessica had looked out the Fowlers' kitchen window. She'd had to admit that it *did* look a little spooky. But she certainly hadn't needed Steven to come over and escort her home. He would have teased her about being a baby for the next two years.

"I'll be fine," she had insisted again to her mother. "Don't send Steven. There's nothing to worry about. I swear."

Creak, creak.

Jessica's heart began to thud against her ribs. Something was definitely behind her. Something that squeaked. Maybe riding home by herself wasn't such a great idea after all.

She glanced over her shoulder again and caught a flash of something large and bulky. *It's just someone on a bike*, she told herself. *Big deal. Just because he's behind me doesn't mean he's following me.*

Creak, creak.

Jessica caught her breath. *But does he have to ride behind me the* whole *way home? Why can't he turn or something?*

Jessica's heart beat faster as she admitted to herself that she'd been hearing that noise from the minute she had coasted down the Fowlers' long, steep driveway. It was almost as if somebody had been waiting for her.

Could that somebody be stalking her?

Abruptly, and without signaling, Jessica turned the corner onto Elm Street, bracing herself to find out whether the stranger was following her. She pedaled several yards, keeping her head down and listening nervously.

Creak, creak.

Here he came.

So what? That still didn't prove anything. Maybe whoever it was lived on Elm Street.

Jessica took some deep breaths and forced herself to stay calm. When she reached the end of the block, she took another right, onto Oak.

Creak, creak.

Jessica's breath caught in her throat. *Stay calm. Stay calm,* she ordered herself. But she began to pedal faster as she took a left onto Evergreen.

Creak, creak, creak.

The man behind her was pedaling faster now, too.

Jessica stood on her pedals as she rode uphill. *Faster, faster,* she commanded herself.

Creak, creak, creak, creak.

The man behind her was stronger than she was. While she struggled up the hill, he was able to gain a few yards. He was getting closer.

Jessica swallowed hard as she took a left.

Creak, creak, creak.

The bike behind her turned left, too.

Jessica's legs were shaking, but she forced herself to keep pedaling as she turned right, back onto Elm. *Please don't follow me,* she pleaded mentally. *Please don't follow me.*

Creak, creak, creak, creak, creak, creak.

He was following her. And he was closer now. Instinctively, Jessica turned her head. As soon as she did, she shrieked in horror at what she saw.

It was a man. A big man.

A man who had no head!

Jessica pedaled wildly, bumping her bike up the curb and cutting across a lawn.

The Headless Biker stayed behind her.

As she flew along, Jessica clipped three metal

garbage cans that had been set out on a curb.

She heard the tires of the Headless Biker behind her squeal as he tried to avoid hitting the trash cans that rolled into the street.

Taking advantage of her lead, Jessica turned into her own block.

The Wakefields' house was almost in sight. Just a few more yards and she would be safe. Just a few more yards. *"Mom!"* she began to shriek. *"Dad!"*

Creak, creak, creak, creak.

"Help!" Jessica let out a terrified sob as her house came into view. She jumped the curb again and pedaled across the front yard. Half falling, half running, she leapt off her bike and threw herself toward the front door, just as the Headless Biker bumped his own bicycle up the curb.

It was a high curb and he almost made it. But the bicycle wobbled slightly. Then she heard a strange-sounding yell as the bike fell over and the huge, headless figure tumbled off.

The Headless Biker, still wrapped in a voluminous canvas poncho and overcoat, rolled across the lawn. Jessica was frozen in fear, her breath coming in gasps as she listened to his strange wheezing noises.

He was . . . He was . . .

Laughing.

The Headless Biker was laughing!

And the laugh had a very familiar tone.

Jessica's hands were shaking. Her head was

shaking. And her legs were shaking. But that didn't stop her.

She stomped toward the figure, reached down and grabbed it by the coat, and began to shake it like a rat.

"Steven Wakefield," she shouted, "come out of there so I can kill you!"

Steven's hysterical laugh turned to deep guffaws. As he rolled around on the grass, she realized there wasn't one person in the overcoat. There were two.

So my stupid brother has his friend Joe Howell in there with him, Jessica thought angrily. "*Both* of you come out," she ordered.

A hand reached through the front and undid the buttons. Steven's head emerged first. He had been sitting on the shoulders of another guy. A guy with dark, wavy hair and deep-green eyes. Jessica stared at him in amazement. He had to be the cutest guy she had ever seen.

Suddenly she realized who he was. She had seen his picture on posters advertising the Skeletons, one of the best party bands in town. All the musicians were students at Sweet Valley High School and super cute. Jessica had always thought that this guy, Scott, the lead singer and guitarist, was the cutest. In person, he was even more incredible-looking.

Jessica felt her mouth opening and closing, but she couldn't think of anything to say.

Scott jumped to his feet as he and Steven untangled themselves. "Listen, I'm really sorry," he said to Jessica. "Steven said you'd think it was funny. He said you were tough—and you sure are. Kept your head and made sure you were being followed before you pushed the panic button. That's better than I would do." He looked at her with admiration.

Jessica's mouth opened and closed a few more times.

"By the way, I'm Scott Timmons," he said.

"I know . . ." she managed breathlessly. "I mean, I've seen your name on posters."

Steven began laughing again, and Jessica glared at him. *What's so hysterical about scaring me out of my mind?* she felt like screaming at him. But she didn't. She glanced at Scott, cleared her throat, and casually tossed her hair off her shoulders. "Pretty funny joke, you guys," she said, forcing a laugh.

Steven didn't say anything because he was too busy clutching his stomach and rolling on the ground, laughing hysterically. "Mom!" he wheezed in an obnoxious imitation of her. "Dad! Heeelllppp!"

"Shut up, Steven," Jessica said angrily. "If you think—" Then she shut her mouth. Yelling at Steven wouldn't exactly make her look calm and collected in Scott's eyes.

Scott touched her forearm. "Don't pay any attention to him. My older brother used to make my life miserable when I was thirteen, too."

Thirteen! Jessica stood up a little straighter.

Scott Timmons thought she was thirteen!

"Try twelve," Steven corrected damply as he got to his feet.

"You're twelve?" Scott asked in surprise.

Big Mouth, Jessica thought, narrowing her eyes at Steven.

"Man, and I thought you were brave for thirteen," Scott went on. "For twelve, you're even more amazing." He smiled again. "Hey, I hope there're no hard feelings about our little prank. Friends?"

Jessica nodded dumbly. Scott was incredibly cute *and* incredibly nice.

Scott turned to Steven. "Thanks for the notes, Steven. See you at school."

Steven dusted the seat of his jeans with his hands. "Yeah, see you. Thanks for the ride," he joked.

"Good night," Jessica managed to call out as Scott pedaled away.

"'Bye," he called back as he disappeared into the night.

Jessica raised an eyebrow at Steven. "How do *you* know Scott Timmons?"

"What's that look for?" Steven asked innocently. "He's in my English class. He came over tonight to borrow some notes from a class he missed on *The Legend of Sleepy Hollow.* You know, the story about The Headless Horseman? Our English teacher thought it would be cool, since Halloween is coming up."

"Yeah, very cool," Jessica said. "I guess you also thought it was cool to *play* Headless Horseman."

"Hey, complain to Mom," he protested. "She made us go over to the Fowlers' and follow you home. She was worried because of the fog." He smacked his hand over his mouth. "Oops. That's supposed to be a secret. We were only supposed to let you know we were there if you got in trouble."

"Gee, thanks so much for rescuing me from danger, brother dear," Jessica said.

"Hey, you forgave Scott in a split second. Why are you still mad at me?" Steven asked.

Because there's a difference between Steven and Scott, Jessica thought. *Scott's a major stud.*

Jessica felt her stomach flutter, but not from fear. It felt more like a serious crush.

"I can't believe they did that to you, Jess. I would have been scared out of my mind if a guy with no head had been following me on my bike," Elizabeth said.

"I was pretty scared, too," Jessica admitted, unzipping her jacket and plopping herself down on top of Elizabeth's bed.

"It's funny," Elizabeth said. "When I met Scott this afternoon, he didn't seem like the type to play mean tricks."

Jessica's eyebrows shot up. "No fair—you got to be home while Scott was here? Weren't you supposed to be at that shack-building thing?"

"It's called Houses for the Homeless, Jess," Elizabeth said, rolling her eyes, "and we quit early because of the fog."

Elizabeth had told her twin about her work at Houses for the Homeless at least ten times, but her twin never quite got the facts straight. It was a volunteer organization that built houses for families that didn't have permanent homes. Sweet Valley Middle School gave students extra credit for participating in the program, but Elizabeth volunteered because the work was really important to her.

"Right," Jessica said absently. "Houses for the Homeless."

Elizabeth gathered up the pile of dirty work clothes on the floor and took them to her laundry basket in the bathroom. "By the way," she called to Jessica. "Have you seen my blue sweatshirt?"

"What blue sweatshirt?" Jessica asked.

"My *favorite* blue sweatshirt that mysteriously disappeared about a week ago?"

"Haven't seen it," Jessica answered.

Elizabeth peered into Jessica's laundry basket. Her sister had a habit of "borrowing" Elizabeth's favorite clothes and forgetting about them. After fishing around for a few seconds, she pulled out the blue sweatshirt, which was all tangled up with a big ball of Jessica's laundry. Elizabeth began to separate the pieces and found another piece of her clothing Jessica had swiped: a T-shirt that had a colorful Southwestern pattern on the front. The shirt reminded her of something she wanted to ask Jessica.

"Hey, Jess, who was that girl you were talking to in the hall before fifth period?" she called.

"The girl with the beaded necklace?" Jessica asked. "Her name is Kala. She's in my math class and she's new. But she said her family is only staying in Sweet Valley for about a month. Her dad's job keeps them moving around a lot. He's overseas now, but when he gets back, they're moving to Los Angeles. Right now she and her mom are staying here with her mom's sister."

"I saw her sitting by herself at lunch," Elizabeth said, walking back into her bedroom with her blue sweatshirt. "I was going to invite her to sit with me and Amy and Maria, but she left the cafeteria before I had a chance."

"You'd probably like her," Jessica said in a preoccupied tone. "She's into educational TV. Documentaries and stuff."

Elizabeth could tell from her sister's tone of voice that Jessica had no interest at all in educational TV or documentaries.

Elizabeth and Jessica were identical twins, but their similarities were all on the outside. The girls had the same, long sun-streaked blond hair, the same blue-green eyes, and the same smile that produced a dimple in their left cheek. But on the inside they were as different as night and day.

Jessica loved parties and gossip and clothes and

boys. She spent most of her free time with her friends in the exclusive Unicorn Club. The other Unicorns loved shopping and talking about boys as much as she did.

Elizabeth's interests were much more serious. She loved reading, writing, and serving as the editor-in-chief of the *Sixers*, the official sixth-grade newspaper at Sweet Valley Middle School. She was also interested in things like educational TV and documentaries.

"Don't you think Scott Timmons is the best-looking guy you've ever seen?" Jessica gushed.

Elizabeth smiled. Obviously, Jessica was too preoccupied with Scott Timmons to give much thought to Kala. "He's in high school, Jess. Don't get carried away," Elizabeth warned.

"If only there were some way I could see him again," Jessica said dreamily, as if she hadn't even heard Elizabeth's advice. "Did I mention that Scott told me I was brave?"

Elizabeth didn't know whether to laugh or groan. Jessica was always getting a crush on some high school guy or rock star. And Scott Timmons was sort of both. He wasn't famous all over the country, but the Skeletons were pretty famous around Sweet Valley.

"I just wish some of the other Unicorns could have been there to see me talking to him. They would have been dying of jealousy. Especially Lila."

"Yeah, I'm sure they would have," Elizabeth said.

Despite the fact that the Unicorns considered themselves the prettiest, most popular, and all-around coolest girls at Sweet Valley Middle School, Elizabeth had no interest in joining. Jessica had tried to talk her into it a long time ago, but Elizabeth thought they were silly, snobby, and self-centered. Worst of all, they were very undependable—which reminded her of something she wanted to ask Jessica. "Was Janet Howell sick today?"

"No," Jessica said in surprise. "Why do you ask?"

"Because she was on the Houses for the Homeless sign-up sheet today. She volunteered to be a bricklayer, but she never showed up."

Jessica shrugged. "I guess she decided she didn't need the extra credit. I don't see why you need any extra credit, either," she added. "You have an A average."

"Extra credit isn't the only reason to help out, Jess," Elizabeth responded. "I signed up because I like the work and I think it's a really good cause."

"I'm sure Janet thinks so, too," Jessica said defensively. "But we had an emergency meeting of the Unicorns this afternoon."

"What kind of emergency?" Elizabeth asked suspiciously.

"Ellen Riteman said she thought we should change our official club color from purple to orange and black in honor of Halloween. So of course we had to talk it over and take a vote."

Elizabeth stared at her sister in disbelief. "Jessica!" she said impatiently. "That's not a good reason for Janet not to show up."

"I think Janet's old enough to decide what's important and what's not," Jessica replied haughtily. "She is in the eighth grade, you know."

Elizabeth rolled her eyes. Janet Howell was the founder and president of the Unicorn Club, and she seemed to think that made her president of the universe. "You really amaze me," Elizabeth said in exasperation. "I can't believe you and the Unicorns could even argue that deciding what color to wear is more important than building houses for the homeless!"

"You're the one who's arguing," Jessica countered. "Why do you have to turn every conversation into an I Hate the Unicorns festival?"

"I don't hate the Unicorns," Elizabeth protested.

"You do too," Jessica said, tossing her hair impatiently. "And anyway, I'm trying to talk to you about the greatest guy in the whole world and you just change the subject to something totally irrelevant."

"Totally irrelevant?" Elizabeth demanded.

"Yeah," Jessica said, hopping up from the bed. "I really need a plan to get Scott's attention, and you're not helping at all. I guess I'll just have to come up with one on my own."

Jessica turned and flounced out of the room, slamming the door shut behind her.

Elizabeth sat down on the edge of her desk chair and sighed. She had a bad feeling in the pit of her stomach. *I think I'm coming down with a case of Jessica-itis,* she thought.

Whenever Jessica developed a new crush, her wild imagination began working faster than ever, planning outrageous and elaborate plans to get what she wanted. And somehow, in spite of her determination not to, Elizabeth always got tricked into helping her.

Elizabeth looked at the wall calendar that hung over her desk. The picture for October was of a whole group of monsters, ghosts, witches, and skeletons. All of them wore ghastly mocking smiles. "Trick or Treat," read the caption.

A chill went up Elizabeth's spine. Whatever Jessica was planning, Elizabeth hoped it would be a treat, and not a trick. Halloween tricks had a way of going too far.

And so did Jessica's stunts.

Two

◇

Elizabeth fastened the snaps on the clean white painter's overalls she wore over an old T-shirt. It was Tuesday afternoon, about twenty minutes after the final bell had rung, and she was changing into her work clothes in the school bathroom. She wanted to go directly to the Houses for the Homeless construction site without stopping at home first.

Elizabeth looked at her watch. *Three thirty already,* she thought. *I'd better move it.* Stopping by the library after her last class must have taken longer than she'd thought.

She quickly folded up the plaid skirt and green turtleneck she had worn all day at school.

As she rummaged around in her backpack, her hairbrush fell out and hit the floor, making a clatter that reverberated through the empty girls' bathroom.

It was strange how different the bathroom felt when there weren't girls hurrying in and out or standing at the mirror. Elizabeth shivered. The place felt so cold and empty. As she walked to the door, her footsteps made a strange, echoing sound on the tile floor.

Elizabeth felt a little nervous flutter in her stomach as she stepped out into the hallway. She didn't like being around the school when it was this deserted. There was something almost *spooky* about it.

"Ohhhhhh!"

Elizabeth jumped. Who was making that groaning noise? She looked both ways down the hall, but she didn't see a soul.

"Hello?" she called out in a tentative voice.

No one answered.

Elizabeth shook her head. Maybe she was imagining things. She had probably heard the central air-conditioning system starting up. Sometimes it made strange noises.

As she walked down the hall, she looked at the black cat cutouts, pumpkins, skeletons, monster masks, and vampire drawings that were pinned up along the walls as Halloween decorations.

"Who wouldn't start imagining things with all this stuff hanging around?" she muttered.

"Ohhhhhhhh!" came the noise again.

Elizabeth stopped. That was no imaginary sound.

It was the sound of somebody in terrible pain. A frightening, horrible sound.

Her heart began a slow, sickening thud. "Hello?" she called out, her voice trembling. "Is anybody there?"

She waited, straining to listen for any signs of activity. But the whole building seemed silent and completely deserted.

Elizabeth began hurrying toward her locker. She was going to get her books and get out of here. She reached her locker, spun the combination, and—

"*Heeelp!*" somebody groaned.

Elizabeth let out a little shriek of alarm and dropped her books.

Whoever was making that sound was on the other side of the lockers.

Her heart hammering, Elizabeth began to creep around the corner to see who, or what, was making that noise.

"*Aaahhhhhh!*"

At the sound of the terrified scream, Elizabeth dashed around the corner. To her utter amazement, she saw Kala staring down in horror at Jake Hamilton.

Jake Hamilton was a cute seventh-grade boy, who wasn't looking very cute at all. In fact, he looked as if he was practically dead.

Jake lay facedown on the floor with an ax embedded in his back. Blood soaked the back of his shirt and trailed along the floor. He was moving slowly, dragging himself along the hall with his fingertips. "Hellllllp meeeee," he moaned. "Heeeelllp!"

The new girl wrung her hands, and she began to sob.

"Heeeelp," Jake repeated in a strangled voice.

Kala put her hand over her mouth, as if she were going to be sick.

Quickly, Elizabeth reached down and grabbed the ax handle. She jerked it up and threw it against the wall, where it bounced away with a *boing*.

"Very funny, Jake," Elizabeth said sourly. "Rubber axes are right up there with plastic vomit."

Jake sat up. "You're no fun," he complained. "Fake blood is expensive. You could at least pretend to be scared."

From the other side of the lockers, Elizabeth heard snickering. She dashed around just in time to catch sight of Bruce Patman and Rick Hunter disappearing into the boys' bathroom.

"Oh, very funny!" Elizabeth shouted.

When she came back around the corner, Jake was grinning and taking bows. "Thank you. Thank you. Ladies and gentlemen, that concludes the entertainment portion of our evening."

Elizabeth noticed that Kala didn't look entertained at all. She looked miserable. She wiped away tears.

"Cut it out, Jake," Elizabeth said quickly. She swiftly picked up the ax and moved forward in a comic menacing gesture. "Now, get lost, or I'll let you have it for real."

She smiled at Kala and made a face, trying to reassure her. She knew that if Jake saw Kala crying, he might tease her.

Jake grinned at Elizabeth and backed away. "You wouldn't really. Come on, Elizabeth . . ."

"Lizzie Wakefield took an ax," Elizabeth chanted in a low voice, "and gave Jake Hamilton forty whacks. When she saw what she had done, she gave *Bruce and Rick forty-one!*" she finished with a shout.

Some muffled laughter broke out again on the other side of the lockers. Bruce and Rick must have sneaked back out of the boys' bathroom and eavesdropped from the other side of the lockers.

Jake began to laugh hysterically, practically doubling over as he ran to join Bruce and Rick. The next thing Elizabeth heard was three sets of feet running down the hall toward the front door.

"Good," she said. "They're gone." She pulled a tissue from her backpack and turned to Kala with a sympathetic face. "It's OK, it was just a joke," she comforted her. "A really stupid, immature joke."

"Why would they play a joke like that on *me*?" the girl asked tearfully.

"Don't take it personally. It's not just on you. The boys consider everybody fair game around this time of year. They weren't trying to be mean. Really."

Kala looked doubtful.

"Just ask my sister, Jessica. My brother and a friend of his played the same kind of trick on her yesterday."

The girl smiled. "I thought you *were* Jessica. I met her yesterday, and she told me she had an identical twin. She wasn't kidding. You guys are so identical it's scary."

Elizabeth laughed. "I'm Elizabeth, by the way."

"My name is Kala," the girl answered.

"That's a pretty name," Elizabeth commented.

"Thanks. It was my grandmother's name. She was Native American."

"Wow. That means you're part Native American. Do you know what tribe she was from?" Elizabeth asked eagerly.

"Yeah, the Nookta tribe," Kala replied. "She grew up in northern California. My family has moved around a lot because of my father's job. But next summer, he and I are going to make it our own family research project to see what we can find out about our ancestors. I saw a documentary TV program about some people in Kansas who did that. They found out all kinds of stuff that they didn't know about their heritage."

Elizabeth had a hard time keeping a straight face. So *that's* where Jessica's "educational TV" remark had come from.

"How will you do the research?" Elizabeth asked.

"We'll drive around the state, visit all the historic sites, and look through archives to see if we can trace our ancestry. In the meantime"—Kala gestured toward the blue beads she wore around her neck—"I like to wear things like this in honor of my heritage. I've started a collection of Native American jewelry and boots and stuff like that."

Elizabeth looked at Kala's jewelry. Even without it, Kala would have looked like a Native American. She had long straight black hair and pretty, almond-shaped brown eyes. Her delicate brows arched toward her hairline like wings on either side of her wide forehead.

"That sounds really neat," Elizabeth said with a smile. "You should meet Jack Whitefeather."

"Who's he?" Kala asked.

"He's one of the project chairmen at this organization I work for called Houses for the Homeless. He's Native American."

"What's Houses for the Homeless?" Kala asked.

Elizabeth quickly told Kala about the group.

"What a great thing to do!" Kala exclaimed. "Would anybody mind if I helped?"

"*Mind?* You've got to be kidding," Elizabeth said. "We can always use another pair of hands. If you want to, you can come with me this afternoon. They'll find you some overalls at the construction site."

"That sounds great," Kala said, smiling. "Let's go."

*   *   *

"You missed a spot," Maria said.

"A spot on me, or a spot on the wall?" Elizabeth joked.

Kala and Maria laughed. The painting had gone well, but Kala, Elizabeth, and Elizabeth's friend, Maria Slater, were all covered with white paint from head to toe.

There were lots of kids and adults working on the neat one-story house that Houses for the Homeless had built from the foundation up. The site was in the middle of an old neighborhood right next to downtown Sweet Valley. One side of the neighborhood was bordered by a busy boulevard, and the other side was bordered by a highway overpass that led into the heart of downtown.

Most of the houses in the neighborhood had been abandoned and had fallen into disrepair. Houses for the Homeless was gradually rebuilding the neighborhood and helping new families to settle in.

"Who are all those kids?" Kala asked, gesturing toward a group of children sitting in a circle a few yards away. One of the adults was showing them how to make collages from twigs.

"They're Nature Scouts," Elizabeth said. "Unfortunately, they don't have a clubhouse." She gestured all around her with her paintbrush. "They don't have a lot of nature, either. They're lucky to have found those twigs."

"Some of these kids have spent their whole life in the middle of downtown Sweet Valley," Maria explained. "That's where the town shelters are."

"That's sad," Kala said. "Little kids really need to get outdoors and learn about nature firsthand instead of just reading about it in a book."

"Yeah, you're right. I wish we could find a place where they could have campouts and hikes and . . ." Elizabeth broke off when she saw Jack Whitefeather walking in their direction. "Hey, look, there's Jack," she said to Kala. "He's the man I wanted you to meet."

Jack Whitefeather was a tall, handsome man in his forties. He wore a Los Angeles Dodgers baseball cap. A long black braid hung down his back. He gave the girls a broad smile. "How are you guys doing over here?" he said as he approached them.

"Hi, Jack," Elizabeth said. "This is Kala. She's going to school with us while her family's in town for the next month."

"Nice to meet you," Kala said to Jack. "Elizabeth told me you're Native American. So am I."

"Oh, really?" Jack responded with a smile. "Which tribe?"

"Nookta. Actually, my dad and I are going to spend the summer tracing our roots."

"That's great," Jack said. "I've got lots of books and information on Native American history and culture. You, me, and your dad should sit down sometime and see what we can find out."

"That would be great!" Kala said enthusiastically.

"In the meantime," Jack said, checking the clipboard he was carrying, "have any of you seen Janet Howell?"

"I saw her at school today," Maria said.

Jack frowned. "This is the fourth time she's put her name on the list and failed to show up."

Just then, an imperious voice drifted in their direction. "Not there. There. Yes . . . *There!*"

Maria and Elizabeth began to laugh.

Of course, Janet Howell has to help out in her *way*, Elizabeth thought as she watched the president of the Unicorns shout orders at Randy Mason, Tom McKay, and Danny Jackson, three sixth-grade boys who were carrying loads of bricks. Janet was wearing Ray-Ban sunglasses, a pair of flowered painter's pants, and a matching floral-patterned hat. *I wouldn't exactly call that dressed for the occasion.*

"Put them over there with the others," Janet commanded the boys. "Then go get some more bricks off the truck."

"We can't stack any more against that wall," Randy Mason protested.

"Of course you can," Janet snapped. "I watched my dad build a barbecue pit once, and I know from experience that you can too stack some more bricks against that wall."

"Whatever you say," Tom muttered. The boys deposited an armload of bricks on top of a precariously balanced pile.

Crash!

The bricks came crashing down, shattering against the sidewalk and raising a cloud of pink dust.

"Hey!" Jack shouted, running in their direction. "Be careful. Bricks are expensive."

Elizabeth and Maria exchanged a knowing look. "I'd better see what I can do to help," Maria said, hurrying off behind Jack.

"Who is that girl?" Kala asked.

"Janet Howell," Elizabeth answered. "She's an eighth grader and the president of the Unicorn Club. And she thinks that makes her the queen of the world."

"Yeah, she doesn't seem too nice. She said some mean things to me about my necklaces," Kala said in a small voice.

Elizabeth felt a rush of anger. It was one thing for Janet to boss around a bunch of boys who for some bizarre reason listened to her. But picking on a new girl was something else. Thanks to Janet and those obnoxious seventh-grade boys, Kala was getting a terrible impression of Sweet Valley Middle School.

Elizabeth wanted to show her that not all Sweet Valley middle schoolers were obnoxious and snobby. "Kala," she said, "would you like to spend the night at my house on Friday night?"

Kala smiled brightly. "I'd love to," she said. "I'm really glad I met you. I was beginning to think that everybody at Sweet Valley School was totally weird."

Three

◇

"Scott!" Jessica shouted as she saw him coming out of the music shop on Tuesday afternoon. She had wanted to sound very cool and collected, but she was so excited to see him that her voice came out screechy.

Scott skidded to a stop, backed up against the wall of the building, and looked around in alarm as if he expected a speeding car to come hurtling past him.

Jessica's cheeks flushed with embarrassment. "Scott!" she repeated more calmly.

Scott smiled as she ran over to meet him.

"Hi, Jessica," he said. "You have serious lung power. Ever do any singing?"

"Singing? Yes!" Jessica practically shouted. She cleared her throat. *Don't be such a spaz,* she commanded herself. "Yes," she repeated in a cooler tone. "I've done a lot of singing. With a band and everything."

"Yeah, you've got a good look, too," he said thoughtfully, studying her face. "Too bad you're not a couple of years older. We'd try to sign you up to sing with us."

Jessica was practically shaking from excitement. "I can look older," she said eagerly. "In fact, a lot of people think I—"

"Hey, Scott!"

Jessica made a face as she saw her annoying brother Steven and his annoying friend Joe Howell come out of an athletic-gear store. Here was her big chance to impress Scott, and maybe even be asked to sing with his band, and Steven and Joe had to come along and ruin everything.

"Getting ready for a gig?" Steven asked, barely acknowledging Jessica. He pointed to Scott's bag from Sweet Valley Music Supply.

"Yeah, I needed a new E string for the party we're playing tomorrow night," Scott answered.

"What party is that?" Joe asked.

"Jill Hale's birthday party," Scott said.

"Cool. You guys must get asked to play practically every party in Sweet Valley," Steven said.

Scott shrugged. "Yeah, a lot of them."

"So how do you decide which ones to play?" Joe asked.

"We just take the gigs that sound exciting or different," Scott explained.

"Got any bookings for Halloween?" Steven asked.

Scott smiled. "Not yet. We've had a couple of invitations to play, but Halloween is a special night. We're waiting for just the right offer. But when it comes, we're ready. I just got the sheet music for 'Monster Ball.'"

Jessica gasped. "'Monster Ball'?" she demanded. She totally loved "Monster Ball," a duet sung by Johnny Buck and Melodie Powers, two of Jessica's absolute favorite performers. The song was about falling in love on Halloween, and for a second it felt as though Scott had chosen it just for her.

"You like that one?" Scott asked, smiling at Jessica.

"Like it? It's amazing! And the video is so cool," Jessica added, picturing how scary but glamorous Melodie Powers looked in her witch costume. Jessica had watched the video over and over, and she knew Melodie Powers's lyrics and harmony by heart. It would be the perfect song for her to sing with Scott.

Jessica pushed back her hair and gave Scott her best smile. "So do you ever play middle-school parties?" she asked casually.

"No way!" Steven and Joe both said at once.

"Sure we do," Scott countered. "We take any gig that seems hip and fun." He hummed a few bars of "Monster Ball." "I think I've got the melody down. And the sheet music will show me what chords to play on the guitar. Now all I need is the gig and a girl to sing with on Halloween night."

"I could be the girl!" Jessica exclaimed breathlessly.

"Dream on, shrimp," Steven said with a laugh. "You're only twelve, remember?"

Jessica bit her tongue to keep herself from shouting at Steven. Why couldn't he stay out of it? "I can look older if I—"

"Hey, Joe and I are going to Casey's for a soda," Steven said to Scott, cutting her off. "You want to come?"

"Sure," Scott replied. "I could really use a soda after singing all afternoon."

"Speaking of singing," Jessica said eagerly, "I know all the lyrics to 'Monster Ball,' and I—"

"You know, I've been thinking about taking up guitar," Steven said, stepping in front of Jessica. "Is it hard to learn?"

"It's not hard if you practice a little bit every day," Scott told him.

"How long before you can start playing songs?" Joe asked, stepping in front of Jessica, too.

"Actually, you can start playing songs right away if you just learn three or four chords," Scott replied.

"Awesome," Steven said, as the three boys started down the sidewalk.

"I've been practicing the harmony!" Jessica called to their backs.

But the three boys kept walking.

Jessica felt like screaming. It was bad enough that those boys didn't listen to anything she said or invite her to go along to Casey's. But on top of that, they didn't even say good-bye! She glared at them as they walked down the sidewalk. Scott was cute and nice and everything, but it looked as though Steven was starting to rub off on him.

But at that moment, Scott turned and jogged back to where Jessica was standing. "I'm sorry, Jessica. I didn't say good-bye. It was really nice to see you again."

"Y-y-yeah . . ." Jessica said, stunned. "Nice to see you, too." Staring at his gorgeous smile, Jessica felt all her anger melt away.

As she watched the boys walk off, Jessica's brain was working furiously. She *had* to come up with a way to get Scott's attention—and to keep it this time.

Suddenly, she had an idea. An incredibly good idea. An idea that was just incredibly incredible.

"Guess who I saw on the way home," Jessica asked Elizabeth, striking a dramatic pose in her sister's doorway after dinner that night.

"Ummmm?" Elizabeth grunted, her head bent over a textbook.

"Ahem!" Jessica said impatiently. Elizabeth could be so irritating sometimes. She hadn't even looked up from that dumb book.

"Elizabeth!" Jessica finally shouted. "Look at me."

Elizabeth lifted her head and raised her eyebrows

in surprise. "Why are you wearing Mom's old dress?"

Jessica twirled into Elizabeth's room, enjoying the feel of the black jersey knit skirt. The dress had been their mother's years ago. It had been stored in the attic in the girls' old costume box.

"It's my witch costume," she answered. "For Halloween. Don't you think it makes me look like Melodie Powers?" The dress was long and black and drapey. With a few pins in the shoulders and hem, it fit Jessica perfectly. Add a pair of high-heeled pointy-toed boots, and she was sure it made her look fifteen at least.

She twirled over to Elizabeth's bed and sat down. "I saw Scott on the way home, and he kind of sort of suggested that if I were a couple of years older, he'd invite me to sing with his band. Isn't that amazing?"

"Except that you're *not* a couple of years older," Elizabeth reminded her.

"Why do you have to be so negative, Elizabeth?" Jessica snapped. "He thought I looked older the other night. And even you have to admit that I look very sophisticated in this dress. If he saw me in it, he might forget I'm only in middle school."

"How exactly is he going to see you in that dress?" Elizabeth asked. "You're not going to wear it around town, are you?"

"Of course not," Jessica said. "I thought I'd wear it to the costume party."

"What costume party?"

"The costume party I'm going to talk the Unicorns into throwing for Halloween. It'll be so cool that even the high school kids will want to come, and Scott's band will practically beg me to play." Jessica swept her hair up on top of her head. "What do you think? Should I wear my hair up or down?"

"Bet you two dollars the Unicorns won't go for it," Elizabeth said.

"Why not?"

"I don't know. I just think most people would feel costume parties are kind of babyish. They'll think they're too old and mature to dress up."

"Are you kidding? Everyone loves Halloween. Look at all the tricks the guys are playing."

"Tricks are one thing. Costume parties are another," Elizabeth said. "I still say the Unicorns will say they're beyond Halloween costumes."

"Well, that just shows what you know," Jessica huffed. "I happen to know that the Unicorns will think it's a great idea. And since I'm a member, I think I know more about it than you do."

"Too babyish," Ellen Riteman said immediately.

"Babyish?" Jessica exclaimed.

"She's right," Kimberly Haver said. "We're really beyond this kind of thing. When people hear Halloween party, they think *trick or treat*. They think *plastic masks*. They think *bobbing for apples*."

"Gross!" almost every member of the Unicorn Club shouted.

It was Wednesday, and Jessica had called a special Unicorn meeting to discuss the idea of a party. They were gathered in the living room of the Fowlers' mansion, sitting in a circle on the Oriental rug.

"Order!" Janet Howell shouted. "Order! Jessica has the floor."

"I'm not talking about bobbing for apples," Jessica said indignantly. "I'm talking about having the party of the year. A party where we can all wear clothes like models and rock stars. I'm talking Johnny Buck and Melodie Powers. I'm talking about *a Monster Ball!*"

As soon as she said *Monster Ball*, everybody started chattering excitedly.

"A Monster Ball," Tamara Chase said excitedly. "That would be the perfect time to wear my cat suit. Every time I try to wear it out somewhere, my mom says it *isn't suitable.*"

Grace Oliver nodded eagerly. "I've got these really great bell-bottoms. They were my mom's in the sixties. She sewed sequins on them, and I've been wishing somebody would throw a costume party so I could wear them."

"Excuse me," Lila interrupted. "I think there's something we have to consider. What if people think it's really uncool and make fun of us?"

"My point exactly," Ellen said, crossing her

arms. "I personally wouldn't be caught dead wearing some kind of stupid Halloween getup."

Jessica bristled. "If it's cool enough for Johnny Buck and Melodie Powers, it ought to be cool enough for us."

"Hmm," Mary Wallace said thoughtfully, her brow furrowed in a concerned frown. "But would the guys dress up, too?"

This brought on another excited and noisy discussion.

Janet clapped her hands and brought the meeting back to order. "We need to think this over very carefully," she said, looking at the group seriously. "We're the Unicorns and we're the most popular girls at school. If we give a costume party, everybody in the middle school will want to come. On the other hand, because we're Unicorns, we can't afford to look silly."

Jessica nervously chewed on her cuticle. Several of the girls looked doubtful. Mary Wallace and Mandy Miller were whispering to Grace Oliver and Belinda Layton. Ellen Riteman was whispering to Betsy Gordon and Kimberly Haver. Lila and Tamara were just staring thoughtfully into space.

"We need a gimmick," Mandy Miller said as soon as she and Mary were finished consulting. "Something that will guarantee that people don't feel like big losers in their costumes."

A gimmick, Jessica thought as the room fell silent.

Suddenly she had an inspiration. She jumped to her feet. "We'll have the party in a haunted house!"

"Yes!" all the girls shouted at once.

Jessica sat back down and grinned as Mary, Mandy, Betsy, Kimberly, and Grace began talking to one another excitedly.

"Wait a minute," Ellen said loudly. "*What* haunted house?"

Jessica shrugged. "Someplace like the old Mercandy mansion."

"But the Mercandys live there," Janet pointed out.

"Yeah, they probably wouldn't lend it to us for a party," Mandy added.

"What about that old house down by the pharmacy?" Jessica suggested. "You know, the three-story one with the paint peeling off. It's got a FOWLER ENTERPRISES FOR SALE sign in front of it. If Lila's dad would let us use it, that would be a great place."

"That is *such* a cool idea!" Tamara exclaimed. "We could put a lot of fake spiderwebs inside."

"That house looks like it's full of real spiderwebs," Mary Wallace joked.

Mandy laughed. "I know—we could make a whole collection of jack-o'-lanterns and set them on the front porch! We could have a pumpkin-carving contest before the party and give the best one a blue ribbon."

"You mean a black ribbon," Betsy told her.

"This is going to be so much fun," Mary said.

Just then, the Fowlers' massive oak front door slammed shut.

"That's probably my dad," Lila said, jumping to her feet. "Come on, let's go tell him we want to use the house. He'll probably think it's an awesome idea!"

Four

◇

"I'm sorry, girls, that house is just too dangerous. It won't be safe to occupy until the wiring is replaced, the roof is repaired, and the rotten floorboards are fixed," Mr. Fowler said to the group of Unicorns sitting around him at the huge kitchen table.

"But, Daddy, we don't want to *occupy* it," Lila pointed out. "We just want to have a party in it."

"I'm sorry, honey," Mr. Fowler said sympathetically. "It's just not safe. Why don't you have your party here instead?"

Jessica looked around the Fowlers' enormous kitchen. Normally, she'd be pretty thrilled to have a party at Lila's. Mr. Fowler was one of the richest men in California, and he owned tons of property around the Sweet Valley area, not to mention his gorgeous mansion. He and Mrs. Fowler were divorced, and because he felt guilty about it, he gave Lila everything she wanted.

But he wasn't letting them use the house by the pharmacy. And the Fowlers' mansion just didn't look spooky enough for a Monster Ball.

"It's not the same," Lila whined. "Don't you see? We need to have it someplace that looks haunted."

Mr. Fowler chuckled. "I wish I could help you, girls. But I just don't happen to have any spare haunted houses lying around. Tell you what I'll do, though. I'll rent the whole skating rink and—"

Suddenly Jessica had an idea so great it made her spine tingle with excitement. "What about that old one-story house on Sleepy Hollow Road?" she broke in. "The one that's by the woods? I've seen a Fowler Enterprises sign on it."

"Yeah, that place looks totally scary!" Mandy agreed.

"That place *is* totally scary," Betsy said, her face filling with apprehension. "Haven't you heard the rumors about Sleepy Hollow Road? There was even a story in the paper about it a couple of years ago."

"You're right," Tamara Chase said, frowning. "There were rumors that a group of boys saw four skeletons walking down the road on Halloween night!"

Jessica felt her excitement turn into fear. "And one of the skeletons had no head," Jessica added darkly, remembering the story she'd seen on the evening news.

Mr. Fowler held up his hands and laughed. "Hold it. Hold it, girls. Those boys just had overactive imaginations. They'd probably been reading *The Legend of Sleepy Hollow,* and their eyes played a few tricks on them. The moonlight can do that."

"Have you ever been out there at night?" Jessica asked.

"Sure," Mr. Fowler said in a musing tone. "Lots of times. When I was a boy, no one lived in that area, so we used to camp there. It was beautiful then. Completely unspoiled. Full of birds and animals. When the land went on the market last year, I bought it to develop so that other people could enjoy the beauty."

"Daddy," Lila interrupted impatiently, "can we have our party there or not?"

"I'm afraid the answer is no, sweetheart. That land is due for development in a few months."

"Can't we use it in the meantime?" Lila asked.

Mr. Fowler shook his head. "The lot is a mess. All covered up with junk and underbrush. You could get hurt, especially at night when you can't see your way around. The company would be liable, and I don't want the responsibility."

"Daddyyyy," Lila whined, "why don't you ever want me to have any fun?"

Mr. Fowler sighed. "Lila. It's not that I don't

want you to have fun. I'm concerned about your safety."

"What if we agreed to clean the property?" Mary asked. "You know, clear away the junk and the underbrush so that you don't worry about somebody getting hurt?"

"But the house itself is practically falling down," Mr. Fowler argued. "The interior walls are already gone, so basically it's one big room. A shack."

"We can fix that, too," Mary said.

"Yeah," Jessica added. "Janet can be in charge of that. She's had construction experience with Houses for the Homeless."

Mr. Fowler looked at Janet admiringly. "Is that so? That's a very fine organization. I've donated a lot of money to them."

Janet preened. "Oh, yes," she said with conviction. "I think it's a fine organization, too."

Jessica held her breath, waiting for Mr. Fowler to say yes.

"Nonetheless," Mr. Fowler said, "using that property still strikes me as a bad idea. There's an elderly couple living on the adjoining property, and . . ."

"We won't bother them," Janet Howell promised quickly.

"Daddyyyyyy . . ." Lila begged in her most persuasive wheedle.

Mr. Fowler put his coffee cup down and sighed. "OK, OK. But only if you girls promise to clean up the lot, and be good neighbors—to the animals *and* the people."

"We promise," all the girls chorused.

Mr. Fowler smiled. "It'll be nice to see the place cleaned up again." He looked at his watch. "Well, I've got to get going. I've got a meeting across town in half an hour. You girls be careful."

He kissed Lila on the top of her head and left the kitchen.

"All right!" Lila shouted as soon as he was out the door.

"Yesss!" Jessica screamed.

The Unicorns all cheered and high-fived one another.

"This calls for a celebration," Jessica announced. "Slumber party. My house. Friday. Be there or be square." She turned to Mary. "Good move, Mary. You made it happen."

"It was your idea," Mary responded modestly. "It would never have happened if you hadn't thought of it."

"It would never have happened if my dad weren't the richest man in town," Lila reminded them.

So far, so good, Jessica thought happily. *Operation Monster Ball is right on track.*

"Gin," Elizabeth said, laying her cards on the table faceup.

"That's three games in a row. Are you sure you didn't mark this deck?" Kala joked.

There was a burst of raucous laughter downstairs, followed by a few thumps and bumps. It was Friday night, and for the past hour, Elizabeth and Kala had been sitting in Elizabeth's room playing cards while the sound of squeals and laughter filtered up from the living room.

Elizabeth hadn't realized that Jessica was planning a Unicorn slumber party when she had invited Kala to spend the night. Somehow, all the commotion downstairs made their own private get-together seem forlorn and a little lonely.

"What are they doing down there?" Kala asked Elizabeth.

"We could go down and see if you want," Elizabeth suggested.

Kala looked almost scared. "No, thanks," she said firmly. "I don't really want to see Janet Howell. Yesterday at school, I heard her tell one of her friends that she thought my earrings were dorky."

Elizabeth made a wry face. "Tact isn't Janet Howell's best sport. But you can't judge all the Unicorns by her. Mandy Miller is nice. So is Mary Wallace. Jessica's pretty nice most of the time, too. But I'll admit that I may be slightly prejudiced about Jessica."

Suddenly Elizabeth's bedroom door flew open, and Jessica stood in the doorway. "Come downstairs," she urged excitedly. "Ellen Riteman brought a Ouija board. We're going to try to contact the spirits."

"What spirits?" Elizabeth asked.

Jessica shrugged. "I guess the spirits that hang out around Sleepy Hollow Road."

"What are you going to do when you contact them?" Elizabeth asked, laughing.

"Invite them to the Monster Ball," Jessica answered with a grin. "See you downstairs," she called, dashing back down the hallway.

Kala looked a bit wary.

"Come on," Elizabeth coaxed. "Let's go downstairs. They wouldn't have invited us if they didn't want us. And Ouija boards are supposed to be fun."

Jessica's fingers rested lightly on the marker that was placed in the middle of the board. Letters from the alphabet ran along the perimeter of the board on two sides.

The girls were sitting in a circle around the board in the Wakefields' dimly lit living room. To Jessica's left sat Elizabeth. To her right sat Kala.

Ellen sat opposite Jessica between Mary and Janet. Her fingertips rested parallel to Jessica's on top of the marker.

"What are we supposed to do besides sit here?" Jessica whispered. "I mean, staring at this marker is getting kind of boring."

"Shhh," Ellen hushed her. "We have to wait for the spirits to send their message."

Suddenly, the marker began to shake and vibrate. Then it shot toward the S.

"It's working," Kala said with a gasp.

"Shhhh," Janet warned.

The marker slid toward the T.

"S T," Mandy whispered. "It's spelling something."

The marker began to dart crazily around the board, furiously spelling out words.

"'Stay'!" Mandy cried. "It spelled 'stay.'"

The marker skidded over to the A. And then in rapid succession it slid to W, back to A, and then to Y.

The girls looked at one another in silence.

"'Stay away'?" Mary said quietly. "What does that mean?"

"It means stay away," Ellen snapped. "I think we're being warned."

"About what?" Jessica demanded.

"About Sleepy Hollow. We should probably forget about having a party there. There might be evil spirits hanging around the place." Ellen's eyes darted around the table. "And besides, it'll be a ton of work."

"You probably pushed the marker the way you wanted it to go, because you're too lazy to clean anything up," Jessica accused.

"That's not true," Ellen said defensively.

"Is so," Jessica insisted. *I should have smelled a rat the minute she walked in the door with this stupid Ouija board*, Jessica thought. *Ellen's such a whiner. She'll do anything to get out of doing work.*

"I might not feel like doing a lot of work, but that's beside the point. I didn't push the marker around," Ellen insisted. "You'll just have to accept the fact that someone, or something, is warning us to stay away."

"Ohhhh, Ellen," Tamara and Betsy groaned in irritation.

"But what if she's right?" Grace Oliver asked nervously. "What if we really are being warned to stay away?"

"Why don't we all take turns asking the board?" Elizabeth suggested. "If it spells the same thing every time, we'll know that nobody pushed the marker around."

Way to go, Lizzie, Jessica thought happily. She knew it had been a good idea to ask her and Kala to come down.

Janet cleared her throat. "I say we forget the Ouija board. There's a better way to settle this question." Janet looked around at each face, closed her eyes, and took a deep breath. "A séance," she said in a deep, theatrical voice.

Five

◇

"Aha!" Jessica said, standing on a tall stool in the kitchen and rummaging through a high cabinet. She had just found the little votive candles in their glass holders.

"Careful, don't fall," Elizabeth warned as Jessica began to hand down the candles to her. Mrs. Wakefield had bought them a long time ago in case of a power outage.

Tamara and Grace were pulling the dining room chairs into the kitchen and arranging them around the breakfast table. Belinda and Mary were turning out all the lights in the adjoining rooms.

Kala stood at Elizabeth's elbow as she took the candles from Jessica.

"I've never been a part of a séance before," Kala whispered when Jessica climbed down off the stool.

"Me either," Jessica said.

"Will we really talk to ghosts?" Kala asked.

Elizabeth choked on a giggle. "I seriously doubt it. I would think any self-respecting ghost would have better things to do than hang out at a Unicorn slumber party."

"Very funny," Jessica said dryly. But as far as she was concerned, Elizabeth could make fun of the Unicorns all she wanted tonight. Jessica was really glad to have her there. Even though Jessica didn't *really* believe in ghosts or spirits, she did have a few nervous butterflies in her stomach. Elizabeth was the best ghost buster she knew. No spook could stand up to Elizabeth's no-nonsense, both-feet-on-the-ground personality.

"OK, everybody, let's get started." Janet clapped her hands and motioned to everyone to take a seat.

Jessica found the kitchen matches and lit five of the votive candles. She positioned four of the candles around the kitchen and put one in the center of the breakfast table.

She took her chair, and all the girls sat in a hushed, respectful silence. There was a tense, almost electric feeling of expectation in the air.

"Everybody put their hands on the table with their pinkies and thumbs touching the hands next to them," Janet instructed.

"Who died and put you in charge?" Jessica muttered under her breath.

"I heard that, Jessica," Janet said.

"Everybody heard it," Lila said with a giggle.

"Do you want to run this séance?" Janet asked Jessica haughtily.

Jessica looked at the group assembled around the kitchen table. Everyone looked pale and ghostly in the flickering candlelight.

"Well, it *is* my house," Jessica said.

"That's true," Mary said.

"Look, if anybody is going to rouse someone in the spirit world, it should be somebody important—like the president of the Unicorns," Janet said with a sniff.

"She's right," Tamara said. "I mean, asking somebody dead to come back and talk to us *is* kind of a big deal. We don't want to take it lightly."

"I nominate Janet to run the séance," Ellen announced definitively.

"I second the nomination," Tamara said.

"All in favor?" Betsy asked.

"Aye," said everybody except Jessica, Elizabeth, and Kala.

"That means I'm in charge," Janet said in a clipped voice. "So everybody concentrate."

"On what?" Grace asked.

"On the spirit world," Janet answered impatiently. "Now close your eyes."

Jessica closed one eye but left the other one open.

"Both eyes," Janet said sternly.

Jessica sighed and closed it.

"Oh, spirits of Sweet Valley," Janet began to intone.

Jessica opened her eye again—just a little. Janet was swaying back and forth.

"Spirits of Sweet Valley," Janet repeated, "the Unicorn Club begs you to return to the corporeal world for just a few moments."

Jessica looked around the table. All eyes were closed. Everyone was still.

"Spirit world," Janet begged in a throbbing, melodramatic voice. "Make yourselves known to us."

Jessica saw Kala's head make a jerking motion. A shiver seemed to shake Kala from head to toe. Her eyes flew open in alarm, met Jessica's briefly, then closed. To Jessica's surprise, her head fell forward and her shoulders slumped. It looked as if she had fallen asleep.

Jessica looked around to see if anybody else had noticed. But every eye was shut.

"Make yourselves known to us," Janet chanted. "Tell us about Sleepy Hollow. Is there any danger there?"

Suddenly, Ellen began to groan.

"What's going on?" Mary whispered.

"Shhhh," Janet warned.

"Spirit world," Janet repeated again. "Tell us about Sleepy Hollow. Is there any danger there?"

Ellen let out a long moan, then she began to speak in a strange, high-pitched voice. "Staaay away," she said. "It's daaaannngerousssss."

One by one, each girl opened an eye. Everybody at the table was peeping except for Ellen, who swayed back and forth dramatically, and Kala, whose chin continued to rest on her chest.

"It's daaaanngerous," Ellen moaned again.

"No, it's not," Jessica said.

"Pay nooooo attention to Jeeeessica," Ellen continued in a high, whining tone. "She doesn't caaaare if the property is hauuuunted or not—she probably just has some costume she wants to show offffff. Why should weéee do a lot of work so sheeeeee can show offffff?"

Jessica glared at Ellen suspiciously. Ellen wasn't too bright, but every once in a while, she was annoyingly perceptive. "Who's we?" Jessica snapped. "We the Unicorns? Or we the ghosts?"

"It'll take hours and days to clean up that old plaaaaace," Ellen continued to whine. "Don't listen to Jessicaaaaa. We'll wind up doing all the work, and Jessica will take all the creeeeeeedit."

That did it. Ellen was too much of a faker to be believed. Jessica reached over and tickled Ellen behind the ear. Ellen let out a long, high-pitched squeal and jumped out of her chair.

"Stop it!" Ellen screeched. But Jessica kept tickling her until both girls had fallen on the floor, laughing hysterically.

"Stop it, stop it," Ellen shrieked, trying to cover her ears.

"Faker!" Jessica accused.

Ellen let out a series of hiccups and then a fresh outbreak of giggles.

Everybody began to laugh, and all the Unicorns dove toward Ellen.

"No!" Ellen shouted. "Nooooo!" Then she broke down into hysterical laughter.

"Kala," Elizabeth said in a low tone, giving her friend's arm a gentle shake. She didn't see how Kala could manage to sleep through all the noise the Unicorns were making on the floor. *She must have really had a long day if she can sleep through all this*, Elizabeth thought.

She shook Kala's arm again.

Kala still didn't respond.

"Kala?" Elizabeth said a little louder.

"What?" Kala said, sitting straight up and looking around in confusion.

Elizabeth smiled. "You fell asleep during the séance, that's all."

"Did anything happen? Are they all right?" Kala asked, looking at the pile of shrieking Unicorns on the floor.

"Yeah, they're fine," Elizabeth assured her. "Ellen tried to fool everybody by talking in this silly voice. But then everybody caught on and started tickling her."

Kala put her hand on her forehead. "I feel so . . . so . . . strange."

"Strange sick, or strange strange?"

"I'm not sure," Kala said. "I—"

"Girls!" an angry voice interrupted her.

Elizabeth looked up and saw her mother standing in the doorway. She was wearing her robe, and her eyes looked sleepy.

"Stop it!" Ellen was still shrieking.

"*Girls!*" Mrs. Wakefield repeated sharply. "Do you know what time it is?"

The Unicorns all became quiet. Jessica looked up, strands of hair falling into her face. "Oh. Hi, Mom."

Mrs. Wakefield crossed her arms.

Jessica cleared her throat and pushed the hair off her face. "I'm sorry, Mom. I guess we kind of got carried away."

Mrs. Wakefield's face relaxed into a smile. "We want you girls to have fun, but it's late, and Mr. Wakefield and I are trying to sleep. So I'm going to suggest that you call it a night. Now, good night, girls."

"Good night" and "Sorry," the Unicorns called as she turned to leave. They all scrambled up from the floor and began filing into the living room, where their sleeping bags were laid out.

"Do you want to sleep in the living room with the others?" Elizabeth asked Kala. "Or would you rather sleep upstairs in the twin bed?"

Kala rubbed her forehead again. She opened her mouth for an instant but didn't answer. Her eyes looked confused, and her pupils were dilated into wide, deep pools.

"Maybe we'd better sleep upstairs," Elizabeth suggested.

Kala nodded and stood up. "I feel so strange," she said again.

"I'm sure anybody would feel strange if they fell asleep in the middle of a séance and woke up in the middle of a madhouse." Elizabeth shivered as a cold draft moved across her face and neck. The kitchen curtains billowed.

"Go on up," Elizabeth told Kala. "I'm going to shut the kitchen window."

Kala nodded and walked sleepily out of the room.

Elizabeth leaned over the sink. She pushed the thin curtains aside and frowned. *Weird,* she said to herself. *The window's closed.*

So where was that cold air coming from? Before she could locate the source of the draft, the curtains fell still and lay flat against the window. The chill in the air disappeared as mysteriously as it had arrived.

"Do you think séances ever really work?" Mandy asked as she wriggled in her sleeping bag. Elizabeth and Kala had gone upstairs a long time ago, and the Unicorns were still whispering to one another.

"It might have worked if Ellen hadn't spoiled things," Jessica replied.

"It wouldn't have worked," Tamara Chase said. "Séances and Ouija boards are just slumber party games. It's ridiculous to think that ordinary middle schoolers can ever really contact the spirit world."

"How do you know?" Grace asked. "What if there were spirits sitting around tonight?"

"Are you kidding?" Tamara asked. "Do you think spirits would just sit around while Ellen faked it? They'd probably do something to get back at her for faking it."

All the girls giggled again.

"Ayeiiiieee!"

A bloodcurdling scream pierced the night.

"What was that?" Lila and Jessica demanded at the same time, sitting up.

"Ayeiiiieee!"

"It's coming from outside the window!" Tamara practically yelled, clutching the edge of her sleeping bag.

There was a rustling, scratching sound against the window and a series of grunts and moans.

"Jessica," Janet whispered hoarsely, "maybe you should go check what's by the window."

"Me?" Jessica asked.

"It's your house," Janet told her.

Jessica took an uneasy breath and crept to the window. With a shaking hand, she drew back the curtain. She felt an automatic scream rise in her throat.

Two skeleton faces were pressed against the window, peering in.

Janet dove for the light and knocked the lamp over.

"Ow!" Grace yelled as the lamp conked her on the head.

The floor shook as Belinda tripped over the hem of her nightgown and fell heavily on top of Lila.

"What is it?" Mary moaned in terror. "What's going on?"

"We did it," Janet wailed. "We raised the dead!"

Six

◇

Elizabeth sat up in bed and flicked on the light. What in the world was going on downstairs? It sounded like war had broken out. There were screams and crashes and moans and sobs. *Those dumb Unicorns can't stop messing around even after Mom told them to be quiet*, Elizabeth thought.

She looked over to the other bed, where Kala was still sleeping heavily. They'd come right upstairs after the séance, and Kala had been so tired, she'd crawled under the covers in her clothes.

Someone screamed again, and Elizabeth jumped out of bed. *What if something really is wrong?*

She grabbed her bathrobe and ran downstairs.

When she reached the bottom of the stairs, she flipped the switch on the wall. Light flooded the living room, and Elizabeth saw the entire Unicorn

Club huddled in the middle of the room.

"What's going on?" Elizabeth demanded.

"They're here," Belinda wailed.

"Who's here?" Elizabeth demanded.

"Some dead people," Janet whispered. "Don't go near the window."

"Lizzie, it was horrible," Jessica said, pointing toward the far window, which was now covered with a curtain.

"Oh, yeah?" Elizabeth said, not knowing whether to be irritated or terrified. She walked over to the window, grabbed the drapes, and yanked them open across the curtain rod.

Elizabeth had to gulp down a scream. Skeleton faces were pressed against the window, and their hands clawed at the glass.

She took a step backward, almost sick with fright as their bony fingers made a clicking, screeching noise against the windowpane.

"Unicorns beware," said a deep voice on the other side of the window.

The Unicorns moaned.

"Unicorns beware!" an even deeper voice repeated.

Elizabeth stared at the skeleton faces. If they were talking, how come their jaws weren't moving?

Elizabeth hurried to the front door.

"What are you doing?" Tamara screamed.

Elizabeth didn't bother to answer. She couldn't believe she had fallen for such a dumb trick. She flung open the door and stepped out into the crisp night air. "You can cut it out now. We're on to you," she called out.

The sound of laughter came from the direction of the flower bed. Elizabeth reached for the hose that lay coiled by the front steps. She bent over and put her hand on the faucet. "Come out by the time I count to three, or you guys are going to get real wet."

She turned the faucet, and a stream of cold water shot out of the end of the hose. She held it away from the flower bed.

"One . . ." she began counting. Slowly, she turned the nozzle toward the hedge. "Two . . ."

The bushes began to wiggle wildly. "Don't shoot!" a familiar voice begged.

Two figures dressed in skeleton costumes sprang from behind the hedge.

"Steven!" she thundered.

But when the boys pulled off their masks, she caught her breath. "Bruce and Rick?" she said furiously. "What do you guys think you're doing here?"

"Crashing our party?" Lila guessed, as the Unicorns were gathering in the front yard.

"Cute costumes," Jessica said breezily, tossing her hair.

It figures, Elizabeth thought. *The Unicorns totally forget they were scared out of their mind the second the skeletons turn out to be two cute guys.* Although Elizabeth didn't necessarily agree, Bruce Patman and Rick Hunter were considered to be two of the cutest boys at Sweet Valley Middle School. Bruce also happened to be extremely conceited, but the Unicorns didn't care.

"I can't believe these cheesy costumes scared you guys," Rick said.

"Yeah! What made you all so jumpy?" Bruce wanted to know.

"We just thought we'd raised the dead, that's all," Jessica said. "Want some hot chocolate?"

"So let's get this straight," Bruce said, sitting down with his mug of hot chocolate. "You girls are actually going to clear the lot and restore the shack on Sleepy Hollow Road?"

"Yep," Lila said. "My dad is letting us use the property."

"But isn't Sleepy Hollow Road the place where those two boys saw the skeletons?" Rick asked.

"That's right," Jessica responded eagerly. "And one of the skeletons had no head."

"So what's the deal?" Bruce asked. "Why are you guys so psyched to clean up that spooky place?"

"Because we're going to throw a Monster Ball!" Jessica said proudly.

"All right!" Rick said. "I'm up for it. Wouldn't it be neat if the skeletons came out for your party?"

"Yeah," Bruce agreed. "You can't really have much of a Halloween without a goblin or two."

"Actually, we tried to invite them, but Ellen messed up our séance," Lila said.

"Then let's have another one," Rick suggested.

"Cool!" Mary said.

"Only, we should be quieter this time," Mandy added.

"Yeah," Ellen said. "Don't tickle me."

The girls were giggling as Jessica got the candles ready.

"Hey, Lizzie," Jessica whispered when she spotted her sister leaving the kitchen. "Please stay. I may need you."

"For what?" Elizabeth whispered back suspiciously.

Jessica winked. "To help me rattle the table. I want the boys to think there might really be spooks at the party."

"Why?"

"It's great PR," Jessica said. "If Rick and Bruce get excited about the party, they'll get the whole school excited about the party. And if the whole school gets excited about the party, then Scott's band might want to play at the party."

"Boy, you really seem to have it all worked out," Elizabeth told her. "Since when do you think this far ahead?"

"Since I met the cutest, nicest guy in the world. Please help, Lizzie. I bet if Scott sees me in my witch costume, he'll totally forget I'm twelve and ask me to sing a song with him." Suddenly her face lit up. "And just think about it. The Skeletons playing at a party on Sleepy Hollow Road? It's too perfect."

Elizabeth sighed. "I'm always on your side, Jess, but I'm not going to help you pull some kind of phony stunt."

"But, Elizabeth—"

"Take your places, please," Janet commanded in her most authoritative whisper. "The séance is about to begin."

"I'll stay, but I'm not helping you out," Elizabeth whispered to Jessica as they took their places at the large, round kitchen table.

"Concentrate," Janet instructed.

Jessica positioned her knee so that she could jostle the table at the right dramatic moment.

Janet took a deep breath. "Spirit world," she intoned. "Spirit world. Can you hear us?"

Jessica gave the table an experimental bump with her knee. She heard Tamara gasp.

"Is that you, spirit world?" Janet asked eagerly.

"I think it's Ellen again," Grace muttered.

"It is not," Ellen protested vehemently.

"Shhhhh," everybody warned.

"Spirit world, if you can hear us, send us a sign."

Jessica bumped the table with her knee.

"Ellen!" Lila warned.

"It's not me," Ellen insisted.

"Then who is it?" Janet demanded in a dramatic voice. "Tell us who you are, O great spirit from the other side."

Jessica sneaked her foot forward to bump the table again, but this time, another foot came down on top of hers, hard.

"Ouch!" Jessica shouted.

"It's Jessica," Ellen said accusingly.

"Quiet," Elizabeth whispered.

"Oh, this is a waste of time," Mary said, getting up and snapping on the lights. "If somebody's always going to try to fake it, what's the use of trying to contact the spirit world?"

"I still say we should stay away," Ellen insisted. "Nobody wants to go to all the trouble of cleaning the lot. And besides, if any of the stories are true, we could be in real danger."

Oh, please, Jessica thought. *If only somebody sensible would speak up and tell Ellen to knock it off.*

"You're being awfully negative," Elizabeth pointed out. "You've got a chance to throw a party that no one will ever forget. That's worth a little hard work, isn't it?"

Way to go, Elizabeth, Jessica thought, smiling.

"Big talk," Ellen shot back. "I don't see you hurrying over there to help out."

"Hey, this is for your party, remember?" Elizabeth countered.

"Well, if you help out, it'll be your party, too," Jessica suggested eagerly.

"Actually," Elizabeth said thoughtfully, "that gives me an idea. I'll make a deal with you. The Nature Scouts at the shelter need a place to play and have meetings. I'll help you guys clean up the place if you'll agree to let the shelter kids use it after the party."

"That sounds pretty fair to me," Rick said.

Janet looked around the table as the Unicorns nodded their assent. "Done deal," Janet announced.

Just then, the kitchen door swung open and Kala stood in the doorway. Her eyes were strangely distant and unfocused.

"What's the matter, Kala?" Elizabeth asked, feeling a tingle of worry in her stomach. "Did we wake you up?"

"The old ones say they are resting," Kala said in a flat voice. "Please do not disturb them."

"If she's talking about your parents," Bruce said, throwing a wary look toward Elizabeth and Jessica, "we'd better get out of here. Come on, Rick, let's go."

Kala's face showed no response. Her eyes were unwaveringly fixed somewhere above everyone's head. "The old ones are resting," she repeated.

"I think she's walking in her sleep," Elizabeth said in a low tone. "I'd better help her back to bed. Try to be quiet so we don't wake her. They say that's really dangerous."

Elizabeth stepped forward and took Kala by the hand. "Kala," she said softly, "I think you might be dreaming. Would you like to go back upstairs with me?"

Kala nodded her head slowly and deliberately.

"Come on, then," Elizabeth said soothingly, "let's go up to bed."

"Up to bed," Kala repeated in a zombielike voice.

As Elizabeth and Kala left the kitchen, Jessica rolled her eyes. "Looks like me and Ellen aren't the only fakers around here."

Upstairs, Elizabeth helped Kala climb back into bed and pulled the blankets up around her chin.

"Kala?" Elizabeth asked softly. "Can you hear me?"

Kala turned her gaze and fixed it on Elizabeth's face. "The old ones are resting," she said. Then she closed her eyes again.

"Kala?" Elizabeth repeated in a whisper. "Can you hear me?"

Kala's head fell slightly to the side, and her breath became soft and rhythmic. She was asleep.

Elizabeth climbed into her own bed and reached for the bedside light. Was Jessica right? Was Kala faking? Or had she really been having some strange dream that made her walk in her sleep?

Elizabeth shivered. If Kala was faking, she sure put on a good act. At least she'd succeeded in giving Elizabeth the willies.

"So you don't remember *anything*?" Mary asked the next morning in a tone of disbelief.

Elizabeth, Kala, Jessica, and Mary were still at

the Wakefields' breakfast table. There were lots of bowls and glasses sitting around where the Unicorns had left them, and Kala and Mary had both offered to stay and help clean up.

Kala shook her head groggily. "I know I didn't sleep well. And I know I had a lot of strange dreams. More like nightmares, actually. But I can't remember exactly what I dreamed, and I sure don't remember walking in my sleep."

"Have you ever walked in your sleep before?" Elizabeth asked.

"No, I don't think so," Kala answered.

"Very weird," Jessica said, shaking her head.

"Come on," Mary said to Kala. "Let's check the living room for dirty dishes."

Kala nodded and grabbed a trash bag.

"Think she's for real?" Jessica asked Elizabeth under her breath when Kala and Mary had left the kitchen.

Elizabeth bit her lip. Kala had sure seemed out of it last night. And this morning, she had awakened with dark smudges under her eyes. "She sure seems like she's for real," Elizabeth said quietly. Then she stared pointedly at Jessica. "Unless she makes a habit out of overdramatizing—*like some other people I know*."

"Moi?" Jessica asked in a hurt tone.

"Yeah, you," Elizabeth said with a laugh. Then she bumped the kitchen table with her knee and made a low groaning noise. "Woooooo."

*   *   *

"... so I'm not going to be able to work for a couple of weeks," Elizabeth told Jack Whitefeather at the Houses for the Homeless meeting on Monday. "I won't be here to help with the construction, but I think I can make a more worthwhile contribution by getting the Nature Scouts a clubhouse."

Jack nodded. "I think you're right. One of our biggest problems has been finding ways to entertain the kids while their parents are working on the houses. You go ahead with the clubhouse. We'll get along fine without you for a while."

"That doesn't sound too flattering," she said with a smile.

Jack laughed. "It didn't come out right. But if it makes you feel any better, they'll get along fine without me, too."

"Where are you going?"

"My brother is getting married in Chicago, and I'm driving up for the wedding." He smiled proudly. "I'm the best man. The work here will go on without us," he added in a reassuring voice. "Beverly will be in charge while I'm gone. If you have any questions or anything, just tell her. I'll be checking in with her every few days."

"Maybe when you get back, we can all have a big picnic out at the Sleepy Hollow Nature Scout Clubhouse," Elizabeth suggested.

Jack's smiled vanished. "*Sleepy Hollow!*" he exclaimed with a frown. "I didn't realize that was the property you were talking about."

"Is there something wrong?" Elizabeth asked. "I mean, we know it's going to be developed at some point. But even if we only get to use it for a few months, it will be worth it."

Jack looked thoughtful. "There are rumors about that property," he said softly, half muttering to himself.

Elizabeth couldn't help laughing. "Rumors about headless skeletons and ghosts? Don't tell me *you* believe all that."

"No. Of course not. It's just that . . ." He paused for a long moment, as if he were trying to decide whether or not to say something. Then he appeared to think better of it, and his face broke into a broad smile. "Good luck on your project. I'll be looking forward to that picnic."

"Hey, Jack!" a boy shouted from the roof. "What about these shingles?"

Jack turned. "I'll be right there," he answered. "I'd better get going," he said, lifting his clipboard in a farewell salute.

"Have a good wedding," Elizabeth called after him. She turned away and began to climb back onto her bicycle.

"Hey, Elizabeth!"

Elizabeth turned.

Jack had paused on the walkway of the house. "Let me know if you find anything . . . *unusual*?"

"Sure," Elizabeth agreed.

Jack waved again and walked around the house.

Unusual? Elizabeth thought as she rode away. *I doubt we'll find anything unusual there. Most tin cans and rusty bumpers look pretty much the same.*

The vampire never returned.

I never wore the cross of my mother. The knowl-
edge of the existence of a vampire drove back my
natural fears. Even you were for me...

Seven

◇

"It's really nice of you to volunteer to help,"
Elizabeth said to Kala as they pedaled up Sleepy
Hollow Road toward Mr. Fowler's property.

Maria Slater and Amy Sutton were too busy
with school and extracurricular activities to help
out, so Elizabeth had been thrilled when Kala had
stopped her just before her last class and volunteered.

Kala gave a half smile. "It's the strangest thing.
Last night I dreamed that a bat flew into my room
and told me to volunteer."

"What a strange dream!" Elizabeth exclaimed.

"Yeah, it was. Do you think that means anything?"

"It could," Elizabeth said with a smile. "Think
about what's going on in your life. Does your
dream relate in some way?"

"That's a good question," Kala responded, lifting her eyebrows as she considered it. "In my dream, the bat asked me *Who will remember that you were here? What will you leave behind?* It probably has something to do with moving around a lot. We never stay in one place long enough for me to leave any mark. I guess my subconscious mind was telling me that helping the kids have a clubhouse would be a way of leaving something behind."

"You know, I bet you're right. That makes a lot of sense," Elizabeth said, impressed. Kala seemed really self-aware.

"Some of the old Native Americans placed a lot of importance on dreams," Kala went on. "They thought that dreams were visions of the past, or prophecies about the future."

"That's interesting," Elizabeth said as they came to the end of the uphill dirt road that led to the property. "Kind of spooky, even." She jumped off her bike. "Well, this is it."

The girls pushed open the metal gate. Most of the field was overgrown with weeds, but several yards back was the old shack, a dark clump of woods several yards away, and the high wooden fence that separated their own patch of ground from the property belonging to the elderly couple next door.

"Doesn't look very dangerous to me," Elizabeth said lightly. "Mostly it looks like a mess. Did your dream prophesize that you'd find yourself cleaning up a dump?"

Kala didn't answer. She just continued to survey the property through narrow eyes as if she were expecting something, or waiting for something to happen.

Kala's mood must be catching, Elizabeth thought as she realized she was holding her breath. But nothing momentous happened. Elizabeth let out her breath in a long sigh. Ellen Riteman had been right. Cleaning this property was going to be a big job. Everywhere she looked, there were rusted tin cans, trash, old auto parts, and tires.

The sight of the old shack filled Elizabeth with apprehension. It was practically falling down. Could they ever turn it into a safe clubhouse for kids?

How will we ever manage to clean this place up? Elizabeth wondered. It would be one thing if Amy and Maria were there to help out, but the Unicorns weren't too big on follow-through. It would be just like them to get tired of the project in the middle and give up.

"Listen! I hear water." Kala walked toward a rocky bank several yards away. "It's a creek," she called out excitedly. "And the water looks clean."

Elizabeth hurried down to join her. It was the one unspoiled thing on the property. Fresh water trickled lazily along the creek, foaming and bubbling around the few stones and branches that impeded its progress. The flowing water continued along the creek line until it disappeared into the darkness of the twisting woods.

Kala leaned down, scooped up a handful of fresh water, and drank. "Tastes good," she murmured.

"Hey, what's that?" Elizabeth asked, straining to hear voices in the distance. She looked up the bank and saw the Unicorns arriving on their bikes. All the Unicorns except Jessica.

"Come on," Elizabeth said. "Let's go back."

Elizabeth and Kala hurried up the bank. They met the Unicorns at the entrance to the shack.

"What a dump!" Ellen said grumpily. "I can't believe we let Jessica talk us into cleaning this place up."

"It sure is creepy-looking," Tamara commented. "Look how dark those woods are."

"Ahem," Elizabeth said, trying to get the Unicorns' attention. "Hello to you guys, too."

"Oh, hi, Elizabeth. Hi, Kala," Mary said.

"Where's Jess?" Elizabeth asked. "I thought she was coming with you.

Mandy looked around. "She's here someplace. She wanted to look around the woods behind the shack."

"Have you guys been here long?" Mary asked.

"Just a little while," Kala said, smiling at the Unicorns. "We were down by the—" Her voice trailed off as her eyes met Janet's haughty gaze.

"Do you wear your Halloween costume year

round?" Janet asked her, staring at her feather earrings.

Kala's face fell, and an angry flush rose up on her cheeks.

That does it! Elizabeth thought furiously. *It's about time somebody stood up to Janet.*

But before Elizabeth could say a word, Jessica came running frantically out of the woods. "They're following me!" she screamed. "There are hundreds of them and they're following me!"

"Who's following you?" Elizabeth asked worriedly, pulling her sister to a stop.

Jessica's whole body was trembling. "Bats! Bats from the cave!" She glanced nervously behind her.

"What cave? What are you talking about?" Lila demanded.

Jessica tried to catch her breath. "There's a cave back there. I thought it would be cool to check it out. It was pitch-black and really creepy, and when I stumbled on a rock, the whole place came to life. There was this horrible screeching, and hundreds of bats were swirling around me." Jessica shivered and glanced behind her again.

"Jess," Elizabeth said gently. "Don't worry. There aren't any bats following—"

But Elizabeth's words were drowned out by a scream. And then another one. All the Unicorns were screaming, and when Elizabeth looked up she saw something small and black zooming over Janet's head, missing her ponytail by inches.

Elizabeth gasped. She and Kala retreated several steps as the bat circled around and headed back toward Janet.

"It's going for your head!" Jessica shouted.

The Unicorns scattered in different directions, and Janet screamed and lowered her head as she ran.

The bat chased after her, darting left and right, as if it were determined to land in her hair.

"Somebody do something!" Janet shrieked.

Elizabeth's mind was racing as she tried to remember what she knew about bats. She was about to dash forward in an effort to scare the bat away when Janet's foot hit a rusted auto bumper. With a cry of alarm, Janet dove forward into the tall weeds.

The bat kept going, disappearing into the dark woods.

Jessica and Lila hurried to help Janet stand up. Janet looked pale and shaken.

"That was really bizarre," Elizabeth said to Kala as the Unicorns huddled around Janet.

"I—I feel like it's my fault," Kala whispered, looking even more scared than Janet had.

"What do you mean?" Elizabeth asked softly. "How could it be your fault?"

"It's just that I . . . I know this is weird, but . . . I pictured the bat from my dream. I was so mad at her, I wished the bat would . . ." She looked at the surprised faces around her. "Never mind."

Elizabeth stared at Kala. Did Kala really believe

what happened had something to do with her dream? Or was she taking a really strange coincidence and making the most of the dramatic possibilities? Was it really possible to will a bat on someone?

Elizabeth shivered. "Please don't go siccing any bats on me," she teased, determined to lighten things up.

But Kala didn't smile. She just bent over and began collecting tin cans, a worried look on her face.

"Correct me if I'm wrong, but you almost look like you're enjoying all this work," Elizabeth commented to Jessica as she tied the top of a trash bag and set it beside some others. It was late afternoon, and the girls had been working nonstop for the past two hours.

"Well, this is work that'll definitely be worth it," Jessica responded happily. "I mean, it would be totally amazing if the Skeletons agree to play at our party and I get to sing with Scott."

"I hope you get your wish," Elizabeth said, smiling. She dropped some tin cans she had gathered from the ground into the garbage bag she carried with her. "I think I'll see if there are more cans by the woods." But she'd gone only a feet few when she stopped in her tracks.

Someone had been watching her from the woods and now had disappeared in the dark overgrowth.

Elizabeth peered into the woods.

There was no movement. Nothing stirred.

I'm imagining things, Elizabeth thought, shaking away her fear. *All of Kala's talk about dreams and prophecies must be getting to me.*

She had bent down to pick up a tin can that was half buried in the mud when suddenly she heard the beating of heavy wings. A huge, dark, wide-winged shadow passed over Elizabeth's head and continued on, casting its ominous shadow on the sun-dappled ground around her.

Elizabeth gasped and looked upward. Only an eagle could cast a shadow like that.

But the sky was empty.

Where was it? Where had it gone? Elizabeth scanned the cloudless blue sky for a glimpse of the creature. But there were no birds of any kind.

This is too weird, she thought. She searched the treetops along the perimeter of the woods. A bird that large couldn't possibly have reached those trees in a matter of seconds. And there wasn't enough cloud cover for the bird to hide in.

So what had she seen?

Just then, piercing screams rent the air. "Run for your lives! It's a bear!"

Elizabeth ran toward her bicycle, where the other girls were heading as well. *Bats, eagles, and bears*, she thought, her heart thumping wildly. She was an animal lover, all right, but that didn't mean she was prepared to cope with this much wildlife.

*   *   *

"Ellen!" the Unicorns chorused several minutes later in disgusted voices.

"Didn't you ever hear the story about the boy who cried wolf?" Mandy asked sourly.

"I didn't cry wolf," Ellen retorted. "I cried *bear*. Because it *looked* like a bear."

"It doesn't look anything like a bear," Lila argued, folding her arms in front of her chest. "It looks exactly like what it is—the shadow of a big tree stump."

"Well, it looked like the shadow of a bear when it was moving," Ellen said stubbornly.

"I can't believe you actually got freaked out by a tree stump *twice*," Tamara groaned.

The girls were standing near the perimeter of the property, where Elizabeth had insisted upon investigating. At the sight of the tree stump, Ellen had screamed again.

"Well, maybe if you used your imagination," Ellen said defensively to everyone, "you'd see that this tree really does look a lot like a bear."

"Get a grip, Ellen," Janet ordered. "You've gotten us all worked up over nothing. Quit trying to tell us that trees look like animals."

"Yeah, Ellen," Mary said, shivering. "This place is spooky enough without you yelling bloody murder every ten seconds."

"It *is* spooky," Jessica told Elizabeth happily as they went back to their work. "I don't think we'll have any trouble freaking people out once we tell them about this place."

"Jessica," Elizabeth groaned. "Can it for now, will you? I'm not in the mood."

"Lizzie, Lizzie, Lizzie." Jessica draped her arm around Elizabeth's shoulders, steering her sister away from the others. She gestured expansively with her other hand, like a used-car salesman. "You're taking this too seriously. Getting too up-tight. Relax. Take a look around. You know what you're looking at here?"

"A vacant lot full of trash?"

"Nope!"

"The future clubhouse for the Sweet Valley Nature Scouts?"

"Nope. We're looking at the way coolest Halloween party hall Sweet Valley has ever seen. People will be so spooked, they'll dance really close just to comfort themselves."

"If they're not too scared to come," Elizabeth said dryly.

"They'll come," Jessica said confidently. "They'll come because if they stay away it's like admitting they're chicken. Besides, nobody will stay away if the Skeletons are playing."

"How are you going to swing that?"

"I'm working on it," Jessica said, tapping a finger to her temple. "It's all in the master plan."

"Meaning you don't know yet," Elizabeth interpreted.

"Geez, why do you have to be such a downer?" Jessica complained. "Don't I always think of something?"

Yes, and that's what scares me, Elizabeth thought. "Listen, Mastermind," she said, "I'll catch you later. Right now I have a pressing engagement with a bologna sandwich and an apple."

Elizabeth headed for the shack, where she had left her lunch.

"Oh, my gosh!" Mandy exclaimed with a gasp just as Elizabeth passed her and Kala.

"What is it, Mandy?" Elizabeth asked as she came to a halt.

"You're not going to believe this, but I saw a shadow slip into the woods—and it looked like a *wolf*."

"Bears. Wolves. Shadows of the past," Kala said softly as Mandy ran off to the group of Unicorns still collecting trash.

"What?" Elizabeth asked in a low tone.

Kala shook her head. "I'm sorry. I'm remembering the rest of the dream I had last night. The bat said something about a bear and a wolf being shadows from the past."

Elizabeth stared. Had the bat incident—not to mention the bear-shadow incident and the wolf-shadow incident—jump-started Kala's imagination? It would be too weird a coincidence if she had dreamed about *all* of those animals.

"The only thing missing is the eagle," Kala muttered, almost to herself.

Elizabeth felt the hair on the back of her neck begin to rise. "I saw the shadow of an eagle," she said quietly.

Kala looked tired and frightened. "I wonder what it means," she whispered.

"Ohhhh, noooo," Tamara wailed from the shack. "Look at our food."

Elizabeth and Kala hurried over to the side of the shack where the girls had stored their food. The bags were ripped open and food was pulled out and scattered in scraps.

"Could it have been a wolf?" Mandy asked in alarm. "Maybe that really was a wolf I saw."

"It had to have been a dog or a raccoon," Mary said. "There haven't been any wolves around here in years. But we still need to be careful that we don't get close to anything that might bite us."

"I'm not really hungry, anyway," Kala said to Elizabeth as she picked up some of the food and threw it away. "Let's go sit in the shade for a few minutes. My head is beginning to hurt."

Elizabeth's head was beginning to hurt, too. She didn't know what to think about everything that was happening. She had the feeling that she was being manipulated, but she wasn't sure by whom. Or why. Most of the time, she could trace a mystery directly to her sister, but somehow she felt that Jessica didn't have anything to do with this one.

"Here," Kala said. "This looks like a good spot."

Maybe it's the sun, Elizabeth thought. *Maybe the light is playing strange tricks on my eyes, and the heat is playing strange tricks on my mind.* She glanced at Kala's worried face. *Both our minds.*

Elizabeth sat down beside Kala. Instinctively, she shot a look toward the dark trees. She still had the feeling that she was being watched. She scanned the edge of the woods, but there was nothing there.

Elizabeth sighed. *I hate feeling so confused*, she thought, absently picking up a stick and digging in the ground.

"Hey," she said after she had dug for a little while, "I think there's a soda bottle or something buried here. I can't believe there's trash even *underground* in this place." She continued to dig, and after a few moments her stick found the object again. She reached down and brushed the dirt away from something. "Kala! Look!"

Kala bent over and her eyes widened. "It's an arrowhead," she exclaimed. "A real Indian arrowhead. I have a lot of those in my collection."

Elizabeth carefully wrapped it in her bandanna and shoved it in her pocket. "I'll show this to Jack Whitefeather when he gets back. He wanted to know if we found anything unusual."

"I don't know how unusual those are," Kala commented. "In some areas of the country people find them all over the place. But it seems kind of weird to find one *here*."

"Kala," Elizabeth began in a tentative voice.

Kala's dark eyes looked weary and strained. "Yes?"

"Let me know if you have any more . . . you know . . . *dreams*."

Eight

"Jessica!" Elizabeth complained the next day. "I didn't tell you about Kala's dream so you could blab it all over school. I wanted to know if you could come up with a rational explanation."

"I didn't *blab* it," Jessica retorted. "I simply told a few, select people that we had had some very interesting experiences on Sleepy Hollow Road and that Kala had foreseen them all in a dream."

"You told Caroline Pearce, the biggest gossip in school, that Kala conjured up a bat and sicced it on Janet. And that after she had done that, she conjured up a bear and a wolf."

"I didn't use exactly those words," Jessica replied with a smile. "I just told Caroline what you told me and let her big mouth do the rest."

"Rumors are flying all over the place," Elizabeth

told her. "Some people are saying Kala is a witch. Some people are saying that Sleepy Hollow Road is really haunted. And some people are saying . . ."

"All I know is that *everybody* is saying they wouldn't miss the Monster Ball for a million dollars," Jessica said excitedly.

"But this isn't fair to Kala," Elizabeth protested.

"Oh, don't be so naive," Jessica sniffed. "Kala is probably loving every minute of it. I would. She's getting attention from people who normally wouldn't even bother to say hello to her—including a lot of the guys."

As if to demonstrate Jessica's point, Kala came walking down the hall, flanked by Ken Matthews and Jake Hamilton, who seemed to be hanging on her every word.

"That's some turnaround for Jake," Elizabeth muttered. "Last week he was trying to freak Kala out with a rubber ax."

"See what I mean? And it won't take long before the rumors start circulating around the high school. Another one or two days and I think the Skeletons will be calling us," Jessica continued dreamily as she closed her locker door. "Well, ta-ta, Lizzie. Gotta go."

As Jessica walked away, Elizabeth watched Denny Jacobson join Kala's entourage. *If those are all Kala's admirers, I hope they keep quiet about it,* Elizabeth thought. Everyone knew that Lila had a major crush on Jake, and Denny was Janet's boyfriend. *If the Unicorns think Kala is snatching their guys, they won't like it one bit.*

"Wow! We're getting this done fast." Mandy folded her arms across her chest and surveyed the thirty heavy-duty garbage bags, full of trash, garbage, debris, and leaves.

"Yeah, the garbage bags look cute, don't they?" Grace asked, pointing to the orange Halloween leaf bags with black jack-o'-lantern faces on them.

The bags stood by the road in neat rows waiting for pickup by the Sweet Valley Garbage Service, a wholly owned subsidiary of Fowler Enterprises. Lila had called them yesterday and arranged for the truck.

Mary waved her rake. "Now that all the junk's been picked up, it's time for a little landscaping. Let's clear away some low-hanging vines and creepers."

"Don't get too carried away with the landscaping," Jessica warned. "We want it to look creepy."

"And we need to be careful about the birds' nests," Elizabeth added. "There are lots of them in the low branches of the trees."

Elizabeth grabbed a rake and began to clear leaves. Soon she saw a familiar pair of booted feet next to hers.

"Hi," Kala said. "Sorry I'm late. I was talking to Denny Jacobson about his social studies project and I lost track of time."

"Oh, is that so?" Janet called in a nasty voice.

Janet hears someone else say Denny's name, and the whole world comes to an end, Elizabeth thought with exasperation. *It's like no one else is allowed to have a conversation with him.*

"You're sure you didn't just *dream* you talked to him?" Janet asked, staring at Kala through narrow eyes.

Kala looked at Janet in bewilderment. "Have I done something wrong?"

Elizabeth stepped protectively closer to Kala. But before Janet could say another nasty word, Ellen Riteman let out a high-pitched, terrified scream.

Elizabeth looked where Ellen was pointing and clapped both hands over her mouth to keep from shrieking.

One of the large bags was moving—almost walking. And a groaning, growling noise was coming from inside it.

"What is it?" Ellen screamed, as the trash bag walked toward her. "What is it? Make it stop!" She began to run to away, but stumbled and fell. "Get away from me!" she cried. "Get away!"

At that moment, Kala leapt forward across the ditch that separated her from the attacking trash bag and came down right on top of it.

"Ommmph!" came the sound from inside the bag.

Elizabeth watched in astonishment as Kala began tearing and breaking the bag. "Come out of there," she shouted. "Come out."

Finally, a head popped up between the leaves and plastic.

"Jake!" the entire group wailed.

Jake Hamilton was laughing as he climbed out of the bag, rubbing his arm. "Boy! Nice work, Kala. Ever think about trying out for the football team?"

"I can't believe you," Mary complained.

"You almost gave me a heart attack," Ellen shouted at him.

"Don't you realize what a dumb thing that is to do?" Mandy demanded. "Never close yourself up in a plastic bag. You might have smothered and—"

"Hey! Where did that truck come from?" Jake shouted suddenly as a garbage truck pulled away. Jake jumped over the ditch that separated the shoulder of the road from the field.

"What's wrong, Jake?" Lila shouted.

"Bruce and Rick were in two of the other bags!" Jake yelled. "Now they're in the back of the garbage truck!"

The girls ran down the road toward their bicycles. "Stop that truck!" Janet yelled.

Jake hopped on Jessica's bike and took off, leaving Jessica and Kala standing in the road.

Elizabeth hopped on her own bike and took off.

Janet was in the lead, pedaling as fast as she could and urging the group on.

"Stop!" they yelled at the truck as they pedaled wildly up the hill.

"Stop!" they cried as they all went coasting down the other side.

But the garbage truck seemed to be making too much noise for the men inside it to hear them.

The truck turned the corner, and the group turned after it.

Elizabeth's mind was racing. How could the garbagemen have loaded two boys without realizing it? Wouldn't Bruce and Rick have made a racket? Of course they would have—unless they weren't conscious.

She swallowed hard, and her hands felt cold and clammy. *Don't panic*, she ordered herself. *You can't help anybody if you panic.*

Finally, after what seemed like an eternity, the truck stopped to pick up another load of garbage, and two workmen jumped out of the cab.

"Wait!" Janet screeched breathlessly, bringing her bike to a halt.

"Hold it!" Jake and Mary shouted in unison.

"Stop!" everybody else yelled.

The two uniformed garbage collectors stared at the group as if they were crazy. "What can we do for you kids?" one of them asked.

"We need to check all those pumpkin-face garbage bags," Jake said, trying to catch his breath.

"Huh?"

"There are two boys in those bags," Elizabeth said in a shaking voice. "They got in there as a joke—to scare us—and then you loaded them in with the garbage."

One of the men began to laugh. "That's very funny. But believe me, if we'd picked up a bag with a kid in it, we would have known it."

"But they were in the bags next to me," Jake insisted. "I heard them laughing and talking to me from inside their bags before you got there."

The two garbagemen exchanged a look. This time, they didn't look so entertained.

"Kid, are you sure? Because if we open up all those bags and don't find anything . . ."

"Open them up," Jake said, sounding alarmed. "Maybe there wasn't enough air in there and . . ."

"You're right," one of the men said, going pale. "Let's open them up." The man jumped on the back of the truck and began tearing at the bags.

Leaves, cans, rubbish, and garbage spilled out all over the road. Elizabeth held her breath.

But there was no sign of Bruce or Rick.

The garbagemen ripped open the bags faster and faster, racing against time. "This is every trash collector's nightmare," one of them muttered, wiping sweat from his brow.

No one said a word as the moments ticked by. The tension and suspense were almost unbearable. Elizabeth's feet and legs began to turn numb. One bag after the other revealed nothing but debris.

Jake swallowed hard as the garbagemen prepared to slit the seams on the last two bags. His face was white with fear. "They were standing right next to me," he insisted quietly.

His voice broke a little, and Elizabeth put a hand on his shoulder. "It'll be OK," she said softly.

The men began to split open the bags. Elizabeth clenched her fists as she imagined Bruce or Rick tumbling out unconscious.

But nothing came falling out of the bags but more garbage.

Jake exhaled, expelling his breath in a long, relieved sigh. "They weren't in there," he said with a gasp.

"That's right, they weren't," one of the garbagemen said, looking around him exhaustedly. "You kids may think this was funny. But let me remind you that this is our job. Silly tricks like this mean we have to take another two or three hours to clean this stuff up. That means we're two or three hours late getting home. Two or three hours late to have our dinners. Two or three hours late to see our families and tuck our kids into bed."

"Mr. Fowler told us you kids knew how to be good neighbors," the other man added. "Fowler usually knows what he's talking about. But not this time, man. Not this time."

Elizabeth felt awful. But she knew that Jake hadn't been joking. He couldn't have faked that fear. But how could she explain that there really *had* been two boys in the bags when she couldn't explain where they'd gone? "Is there any way we can help you?" she asked quietly.

One man reached into the back of the truck for a long broom. "You kids can help by getting out of our way and letting us get our work done."

"Yes, sir," Jake said quickly, climbing back onto Jessica's bike.

"Yes, sir," they all repeated in subdued voices.

"And the next time you want to get rid of your trash and garbage," the other man added, "don't call us. The dump is that way." He pointed. "About five miles. You can take it there yourselves."

Elizabeth nodded, then turned to the others. "We better get—"

"Hey! What's going on?" It was Jessica's voice.

Elizabeth and the others looked down the road and saw Kala struggling to pedal her bike with Jessica sitting on the handlebars. "Did you find them?" Jessica asked.

Kala rode her bike nearer to the truck. "What happened? What's wrong?"

Mandy sighed. "Let's go back, and we'll fill you in."

Everybody climbed on their bikes and began to ride back. They pedaled slowly this time, and Kala and Jessica were able to keep up with the group.

Just as they came over the hill, Elizabeth gasped and pointed. "Look!"

Standing in the same spot, exactly where the other trash bags had been, were two more trash bags. And they were moving.

*   *   *

Jake pounced on one of the bags, ripping it open, while the girls behind him pounced on the other.

"Where were you guys?" Jake shouted as Bruce's head appeared through the tear in the bag.

"Where were we?" Bruce responded, panting. "Where were *you*?"

Rick Hunter's head appeared through the tear in the other bag. "Hey, I thought the plan was to stay together," he complained, climbing out of the bag. "Why'd you move us?"

"Move you?" Jake protested. "What are you talking about? I stuck to the plan, just like we agreed. Just before it was time to scare Ellen, I whispered 'ready' and you guys both whispered 'ready' back."

"Yeah, I heard that," Bruce said. "But right afterward, somebody picked up the bag with me in it and moved me I don't know where."

"Same here," Rick insisted. "After that I heard a truck and a bunch of yelling, and then everything just went quiet." He brushed some leaves out of his hair and looked embarrassed. "And, uh, this might sound kind of bizarre, but then I heard someone talking in this weird voice. They said, *The old ones are pleased that you are showing respect and cleaning up.* Or something like that. The next thing I knew, I was getting carried again." He grinned sheepishly.

Bruce was shaking his head. "Same thing happened to me, only the voice told me, *Find another place to play tricks.*"

Jake laughed. "Well, whoever moved you, moved you right back to the original spot."

"OK, OK," Bruce said with a grin. "You guys got us good. Whose idea was it? Come on, fess up so we can congratulate you."

Elizabeth looked all around. Everyone looked as confused and relieved and worried as she was. There was something strange going on, but she had no idea what it was.

"Hey!" Jake exclaimed, looking at Kala. "It was you, wasn't it? Somehow you fixed it. To get us back for what happened behind the lockers."

Kala stared at him, unsure of what to say.

"I mean, you were talking about *old ones* the other night," Jake continued.

Bruce began to laugh. "All right, Kala. Two points."

"Yeah, you've really got a demented sense of humor," Rick said admiringly.

Elizabeth watched Kala's expression of bewilderment as the boys congratulated her. *She sure doesn't look like she was behind this prank. In fact, she doesn't look like she has any idea what they're talking about. So what does all that "old ones" stuff really mean?* She shivered as the boys erupted in a fresh burst of laughter. "This whole thing seems kind of creepy," she said to Jessica

"Oh, please," Janet cut in. "What's creepy about some dumb trick? I'm sick of all this 'old ones' business, and I'm sick of spending so much time cleaning up. It's obvious to me that *some* people aren't taking it seriously and are messing things up for the rest of us." She tossed her head and glared at Kala.

"Janet's right," Lila added. "And if people keep trying to make a joke out of everything, we'll never get done. So I say we quit." She brushed off her hands with a look of satisfaction.

Janet looked around at the Unicorns. "We have better things to do than clean up some ugly shack."

"Yeah!" Ellen agreed happily.

"B-but wait! We're not finished!" Jessica protested.

"Yes, we are," Janet informed her.

Jessica threw Elizabeth a desperate look, but Elizabeth just shrugged her shoulders and tried to look sympathetic.

"But—" Jessica protested helplessly.

"I don't want to hear it," Janet said impatiently. "You might as well accept the fact that throwing a Halloween party at this dump was a ridiculous idea."

"But what am I supposed to do about the band?" Jessica blurted out.

"What band?" Janet Howell asked.

"The Skeletons," Jessica said casually.

Mary's jaw dropped.

"You got the Skeletons to play for our party?" Mandy asked in an awed voice.

"Yep," Jessica said proudly.

"They're the hottest band in Sweet Valley," Ellen said suspiciously. "How'd you get ahold of them?"

"Scott Timmons and I happen to be very good friends," Jessica said, tossing her hair over her shoulder.

"Why didn't you tell us?" Mary asked.

"I wanted it to be a surprise," Jessica replied.

"Well," Janet said, folding her arms. "Hmmm."

"The Skeletons!" Lila said excitedly. "They're amazing! My dad tried to get them to play for one of my parties once, but they said they had another gig. He offered them a lot of money, but they still wouldn't play."

"Good work, Jessica," Janet said.

"Very cool," Mandy added.

"I guess we can't call off the party if the Skeletons are playing," Tamara Chase said.

Janet picked up her tools again. "Let's get back to work!"

As the Unicorns picked up their rakes to begin cleaning up again, Elizabeth clutched Jessica's arm. "Tell me you have a plan," she whispered. "Please tell me you have a plan."

"I have a plan," Jessica said with a mischievous grin.

Elizabeth folded her arms. "Really?"

"Well, not exactly," Jessica said. "But I will by tonight."

Elizabeth groaned.

Nine

"Thanks for coming out here with me," Kala said.

"Thanks for asking me." Elizabeth sat beneath a tree and turned her face upward to catch the warm sun.

It was Saturday morning, and Kala had ridden over to the Wakefields' house not too long after sunrise to ask Elizabeth to join her for a picnic breakfast on Sleepy Hollow Road.

While Kala laid out the corn muffins, Elizabeth looked around the property with a real sense of achievement. There were no rusted auto parts, tin cans, litter, or rubbish anywhere in sight. *With a little help from me and Kala, the Unicorns actually did a good job of cleaning it up*, she thought happily.

There was still a lot to do. Some of the trees and vines needed to be cut back. And they hadn't even started to clean out and restore the shack yet. But the work left to be done seemed manageable—as long as Jessica could keep the Unicorns happy by figuring out some way to book the Skeletons.

Kala poured two cups of herbal tea from a thermos. "This is probably pretty close to what the early Native Americans had for breakfast."

"Think they had a thermos?" Elizabeth joked.

Kala smiled. "No. But they had jugs that they could plug with wax and things like that." Kala handed Elizabeth a cup of tea and then took a sip of her own. "Um, Elizabeth, there's something I want to talk to you about."

"Sure, anything," Elizabeth said.

"Well," Kala began in a hesitant voice, "there are a lot of strange things happening, and I don't know what to think."

Elizabeth smiled. "That makes two of us."

"I guess I just wanted to ask you privately if you think Jessica is playing jokes on me. I know that some of the Unicorns think I'm weird . . . or that I'm a phony. I thought maybe that garbage-bag thing was some way of making fun of me."

Elizabeth shook her head. "I don't think Jessica had anything to do with it. As a matter of fact, last night she asked me if I thought *you* were behind it."

Kala sighed. "I didn't whisper anything about 'old ones' to Bruce and Rick—at least I don't think I did. But when they told us what happened, I still somehow felt it was all connected to me. I'm just not sure how. I had another dream last night. The bat, the bear, the eagle, and the wolf were all there. They wanted me to do something, but I couldn't figure out what. They wanted me to 'do something for the old ones.' And they wanted me to do something about this place."

"Do you think the *old ones* are the elderly couple that live over there?" Elizabeth pointed to the fence.

Kala shrugged. "I don't know. Maybe. It seems pretty logical."

"Did the animals say anything else?"

"Well, the wolf laughed. He said to the others, 'She doesn't believe in us. She thinks we are shadows.' Then the bear said, 'We must show her proof that we are not just shadows of the past, we are visions of the future.' Do you think my imagination has gone haywire?" Kala asked bluntly.

"Well . . ." Elizabeth said, deliberating over her answer. Suddenly she looked up at the sound of grinding gears. A large, lumbering utility vehicle was working its way slowly up Sleepy Hollow Road. When it reached the gate, the driver got out and beckoned them over.

"I wonder what's up," Elizabeth said as she and Kala stood up and made their way across the field.

"Can we help you?" Elizabeth asked as soon as they got within earshot.

The man was wearing a hard hat and had a bandanna wrapped around his neck. "Good morning. Mr. Fowler asked me to come out here and talk to some . . ." He cocked his head as if he was trying to remember what he had been told. "Not zebras," he muttered. "Horses? . . . Ummmm . . . Nope." He scratched his chin in perplexity.

"Unicorns?" Elizabeth suggested helpfully.

The man snapped his fingers. "That's it exactly." The man wiped his hand on the sleeve of his jacket and extended it to shake. "I'm Joe Cartrain, head contractor for Fowler Construction. We're planning to build a twenty-story office tower on this land. Problem is, the start date has been pushed up, and that means we'll need to start almost immediately."

"Immediately?" Elizabeth and Kala said at once.

The man nodded. "No later than November second." He looked around the property. "Mr. Fowler said you girls were using the shack for some kind of party or something, but it'll have to go. When we clear this lot, we'll knock down that shack and probably a good fifteen feet of trees, too."

"Darn," Kala said in a low voice. "There goes the Nature Scout clubhouse."

"Nature Scout clubhouse?" the man repeated.

Elizabeth nodded. "We had hoped that we could use the shack as a Nature Scout clubhouse for the kids from the homeless shelter."

Kala looked around. "It's such a beautiful place, too. I hate to think of it covered with an office building."

The man smiled. "I know you're disappointed, but you don't have to worry—the place won't be destroyed. It'll be one of the most beautiful office parks in Sweet Valley. Go down to Mr. Fowler's office one day and look at the model. It looks great. An office building surrounded by trees. We're going to put some stone tables out by the water so workers can have picnic lunches outside."

Elizabeth did her best to smile. The man was just trying to make her feel better, and the building *did* sound nice—for a building. *But so much for having the clubhouse here*, she thought.

The man climbed back into his truck. "Gotta go," he said cheerfully. "Lots of other work to do. So don't spend too much more time fixing the place up. Nobody wants to see you kids waste a lot of your time and effort, OK?" The man winked and gave the girls the thumbs-up sign.

As the vehicle drove away, Elizabeth felt her heart sink. She had grown attached to this rustic area with its wild woods. It was really too bad it would have to be cleared for a twenty-story office building, even a nice one. "I guess that's it," Elizabeth said sadly.

Kala was silent for a long moment, then she went over and sat down under a tree. She pulled her legs up and rested her chin on her knees. "Maybe . . ." she began.

"Maybe what?" Elizabeth asked, sitting down next to her.

"Maybe my dream meant I'm supposed to do something about the construction. Maybe the old couple next door don't want a big tower built in their backyard. Or maybe Mr. Fowler's company is forcing them off their land. That kind of thing still happens, you know? Just like it happened to the Native Americans."

Elizabeth ran her fingers through the loose soil underneath the pine needles. "I don't know, Kala, that seems awfully—" Elizabeth broke off when her fingers closed over something hard and sharp. She pulled it up out of the dirt and inspected it. "My gosh. I found a tooth."

Kala gasped and her hand flew to her face. "It's a bear tooth," she whispered. "The bear said they'd have to show me proof. I bet this is the proof he meant."

Elizabeth's mind was racing. Was Kala right? Were the animals in her dreams mystical visions? Or was it possible that she was orchestrating an elaborate hoax?

The tooth had been fairly close to the surface of the ground. Maybe someone had planted it there. "I need some time to think about this," Elizabeth said slowly.

"I need to think, too." Kala stood up. "And I need to get some sleep. Would you be really upset if I didn't help out today?"

"Of course not," Elizabeth said. "If we can't use the shack for a Nature Scout clubhouse, there's not much point in your working here." She grinned. "There's not much point in my working here, either, except that I've promised Jessica I'd fill in for her today. She wants me to keep the Unicorns from deciding they're sick of the project. She's afraid they're all going to quit, and I guess I don't blame her."

"Watch it!" Grace shouted as a sheet of dust and gravel came raining down on her head. She was standing inside the shack with her upper body leaning out of the window as she tried to knock down a mud dauber's nest with a broom handle.

It was later that afternoon, and several of the Unicorns were working on the shack. They had been surprised by the news about the construction, but as long as the property would be intact for their party, nobody really cared what happened to the place.

"I said *watch it!*" Grace bellowed.

"Sorry," Elizabeth heard Tamara yell from the roof, where she was clearing away the webs, dust, and layers of rotted newspaper that were up there.

Grace sneezed several times in a row as another sheet of dust and dirt came raining down. When her sneezing fit was over, she looked up toward the roof. "That's the third time you've done that," she complained. "Can't you see my head sticking out the window?"

"Well," Tamara retorted, "if you know I'm up

here cleaning the roof, why do you keep sticking your head out the window?"

"Arggghhh!" someone screamed.

Elizabeth jumped and dropped her broom.

"What is it?" Betsy cried, rushing into the shack with Kimberly right behind her.

Ellen Riteman pointed to the body of a rabbit that had been under a pile of old, rotten plywood. "It's dead," she wailed.

Mary stomped toward it holding a big garbage bag. "No wonder it stinks in here," she mumbled from beneath the surgical mask she wore over her nose and mouth.

Elizabeth sighed and picked up her broom again. She was getting tired of hearing Ellen make such a big deal over everything, but she was glad that at least some of the Unicorns were really working and not just complaining all the time.

"I'm telling you, the best way to reinforce these walls is with Sheetrock," Mandy told Janet loudly as the girls walked inside. "It's quick, and it's cheap. We only need it to stand for one night."

"Obviously," Janet said in a superior tone, "you have not had as much construction experience as I have."

"Make that none," Mary whispered in Elizabeth's ear.

Elizabeth snorted a laugh.

Mandy tapped her hammer against the wall. "If we don't reinforce these walls, they're going to crumble when people get in here and start to boogie."

"I say forget the Sheetrock," Janet argued. "We'll use some of that lumber outside for reinforcement beams."

"But that lumber is rotten," Mandy protested.

Janet folded her arms and sighed elaborately. "*I* am the chief contractor, and *I* know what I'm doing—which means we'll do it my way, or we won't do it at all."

Uh-oh, Elizabeth thought. *This could get ugly.*

She could almost see the Unicorns squaring off for a big argument over which was better for reinforcement, Sheetrock or lumber. And they'd get so mad that they'd all quit—just what Jessica was afraid of.

Elizabeth began humming the opening bars of "The Monster Ball." ". . . get ready for the monster ball," she sang as she mixed up a gallon of whitewash. ". . . it's the scariest party of all . . ."

Mandy smiled and picked up the melody, singing in an alto voice.

Just then, Betsy turned up the music on the boom box she'd brought along. "Hey, listen, you guys!"

"It's 'The Monster Ball'!" Ellen said excitedly.

"Turn it up!" Mandy called.

Elizabeth watched as the Unicorns began dancing and singing along. She had done exactly what Jessica wanted her to do, but somehow she didn't feel relieved. Instead, she felt spooked. That song's coming on the radio just as she'd started to sing it was really creepy. Maybe it was some kind of message. Maybe Kala was right—someone was trying to tell them something.

Jessica fell back a few feet and slipped behind a hedge. She was trying to catch Scott as he came out of the music store, and she was so frustrated she was about to scream. Scott was at the music store all right, but he was there with Steven and Joe, who had to be the two biggest tagalongs in Sweet Valley—or maybe even the world. And there was no way she could talk to Scott with the two of them around. The minute she told Scott about the mysterious stuff that had been going on, Steven would tease her and make her look like a little kid.

She waited for almost an hour for Scott and his groupies to come out of the music store. Then she followed them to the bookstore. After the bookstore, she stood behind a trash can outside the diner and watched the three of them wolf down hamburgers and sodas. She wanted a hamburger, too, but she was afraid if she went in to order something, she'd miss them when they came out.

By the time they left the diner, Jessica was almost fainting with hunger and fatigue. But she still managed to follow their tracks, straining to overhear them.

I'd make a great private detective, she thought as she crept a few yards closer.

"Why don't we go to my house," she heard Scott say to Steven and Joe. "That way you guys can try playing my guitar and see how you like it. And if you want to sleep over we can do some late-night jamming. The garage is soundproof."

No, Jessica pleaded silently. *Say no. Say you're busy. Say you've got a date. Please, Steven, SAY NO.*

"That sounds great," Steven said.

As the three boys rounded a corner and disappeared, Jessica flopped down on the grass with a loud, frustrated moan.

"Let's trim the branches that brush up against the shack," Tamara suggested, pointing to them with her saw. "We should probably start with that tree there. If we can climb it, that is."

"I can climb it," Elizabeth said. She grabbed a low-hanging branch and pulled herself up into the leafy thicket. Limb by limb, she made her way closer to the long branch that stretched over the shack.

It's got a crack, she realized. *It must have been struck in a storm. And it could be dangerous if it fell on the roof in the middle of the party.*

She tentatively put her foot on the branch, testing its strength. It teetered slightly. *Hmmmm. It definitely needs to be trimmed,* she thought.

But when her eyes traveled the length of the branch, she saw a bird's nest.

"We can't cut this branch," she shouted down to Tamara.

"How come?"

"There's a bird's nest in it." As Elizabeth began to climb back down, she heard a slow cracking sound.

"No!" she cried, watching with horror as the long branch fell past her, narrowly missing the roof. As the branch hit the ground, the bird's nest fell out, and five little speckled eggs cracked in the dirt.

The mother bird came flying back to her nest. She let out a series of distressed cries when she saw the damage, and then wheeled around and flew away, disappearing into the dark woods.

"I'm sorry," Elizabeth called after the bird. She sighed and looked at Tamara. "It was an accident, but I feel terrible. If I hadn't pushed it with my foot, it wouldn't have fallen."

Tamara tossed her hair. "Look, Elizabeth, after our party, a big bulldozer is probably going to come along and knock every single thing down. Who cares if we break a few bird's eggs?"

"Yeah," Kimberly Haver added with a laugh. "You can't have a Halloween omelette without breaking a few eggs."

Elizabeth was so angry, she thought she might burst. How could they be so insensitive? *I'd better find something else to do before I say something I'll regret.*

She reached for the nearest sack of garbage. "Where are we stacking these now that the garbagemen won't come get our trash?" she asked Tamara.

Tamara giggled and pointed to the high wooden fence that separated their land from the neighbors' property.

"What do you mean?" Elizabeth asked.

"I'll show you." Tamara took the garbage from Elizabeth, walked over to the fence, and heaved it over. She dusted her hands and smiled proudly. "Any questions?"

"But we're supposed to take our garbage to the dump!"

"Oh, come on, the dump is a five-mile ride from here. Besides," Tamara said, wrinkling her nose, "it smells bad. Don't worry about it, Elizabeth. We're not going to be here much longer."

Elizabeth watched in shock as the girls all grabbed garbage bags and began throwing them over the fence. *Those Unicorns are unbelievable,* she thought, backing up. She didn't want anything to do with throwing garbage on somebody else's land.

A cold wind suddenly blew past Elizabeth, lifting the tendrils of her hair and forming a small whirlwind of leaves and dust.

A bead of perspiration trickled down from her hairline, and the palms of her hands felt clammy. The swirling air made her teeth chatter. Something had caused her to break out in a cold sweat, and suddenly she was afraid.

"Stop it," she whispered to the wind. "I don't believe in ghosts. I don't believe in visions. And I don't believe that something I can't see will hurt me."

The wind died down and Elizabeth exhaled, releasing her tension.

There, she thought. *There's nothing to be afraid of.* Even if there *was* something strange going on, she wasn't going to let it scare her.

She heard someone laughing. *Who's there?* she wondered, looking toward the woods, where the noise was coming from. It didn't sound like laughter anymore. It was a strange barking sound—the kind of sound a wolf might make.

Ten

◇

"Hello!" Kala called from across the field as she rode up Sleepy Hollow Road on her bike.

It was almost evening, and Elizabeth and the Unicorns were picking up the last debris outside the shack before heading home.

"Wow, Kala," Mary commented as Kala got off her bike and walked across the field to where everyone was standing. "You look really tired."

"Couldn't you sleep?" Elizabeth asked. Kala *did* look tired. There were deep shadows under her eyes, and she had the tense, exhausted look of someone who had been sick.

"I did sleep," Kala said. "I slept all afternoon. And I dreamed all afternoon."

Janet rolled her eyes and snorted.

"What did you dream about?" Elizabeth asked, ignoring Janet.

"It's so strange, but I dreamed about the animals again. The wolf said it had a message for the Unicorns."

Elizabeth's skin tingled. *A wolf?*

Janet's eyes darted back and forth between Kala's face and Elizabeth's. "A message for us? What kind of message?" she asked in a tone of forced calmness.

"They wanted me to give you a warning," Kala said. "They said *the old ones are angry*."

"Oh, please," Lila said, tapping her foot impatiently.

"We're really getting sick of you and your old ones," Janet told her haughtily, as the other Unicorns began to snicker.

Why do they always laugh at things they don't understand? Elizabeth thought angrily.

"So, Kala," Janet went on with a contemptuous smile, "what do you think 'the old ones are angry' means?"

"It means the old folks next door found our garbage," Ellen said in a bored tone. "Big deal. What are they going to do? Throw it back at us?"

"Maybe we should go over and apologize," Mandy said.

"Why should we apologize?" Lila demanded. "They don't have any right to get angry."

"Sure they do," Mary said. "We dumped garbage on their land."

Lila smirked. "I looked at the map in my dad's office at home. According to the land map, there's a twenty-foot easement between the two lots. That means that there's twenty feet of property along the fence line that doesn't belong to them." She smiled triumphantly.

"Yeah, but it doesn't belong to us either," Mary pointed out.

"It doesn't matter who it belongs to," Mandy said. "We shouldn't have thrown all that garbage over there just because we were too lazy to go to the dump."

While the Unicorns argued, Kala nervously fingered her earrings and began to back away.

"I'm sorry the Unicorns are being so horrible," Elizabeth said. "If you hang on a minute, we can ride back together."

"No, I don't think so," Kala said. "I guess I thought I had to come here and at least try to give the Unicorns the message. But they don't believe me"—she looked at Elizabeth with hurt eyes—"and neither do you."

"Kala!" Elizabeth protested. "What makes you say that?"

"That was the other part of the dream," she said. "The wolf told me that you don't believe me either." With that, Kala turned, grabbed her bicycle, and rode across the field.

"You never even talked to him?" Elizabeth yelped. It was evening, and she was flopped on

Jessica's bed. "Jessica, Halloween is only ten days away. Everybody thinks it's a done deal. What happens when somebody asks Scott about the party and he says he's never even heard of it?"

"That's a good point," Jessica said, leveling a finger at Elizabeth. "That's a very good point. This is why I need you on my team. You're a great thinker and . . ."

"Uh-oh." Elizabeth smelled a rat. Jessica never showered her with flattery unless she wanted something—something big.

Elizabeth stood up and walked toward the door. "I'm getting out of here."

Jessica jumped up and slammed the door shut before Elizabeth could escape. "No you don't."

Elizabeth laughed and ran toward the bathroom. But Jessica dove across the room and blocked the bathroom door with her arms and legs. "All I want is one itty-bitty favor."

"With you there's no such thing as an itty-bitty favor," Elizabeth retorted. She ducked down, determined to slip under Jessica's arm and escape.

But Jessica ducked, too, and Elizabeth found herself nose to nose with her twin. "OK, OK. I give up. What do you want?"

"I'm going to spend the day tomorrow stalking Scott again. And since you did *such* a good job at the shack today, I need you to take my place again tomorrow. Keep an eye on things. Break up the arguments. You know the deal."

"Come on, Jess, I already put in my time," Elizabeth protested.

"It's for a good cause," Jessica reminded her.

"What good cause? The shelter kids aren't even going to get a chance to use it as a clubhouse."

"Don't you think helping with the Monster Ball is a good cause?" Jessica asked in a wheedling tone.

"No," Elizabeth said bluntly.

Jessica sighed and made her eyes look sad and pleading. "Don't you think helping your sister is a good cause?"

Elizabeth groaned miserably. "Ohhhhh. I hate it when you do this."

"Does that mean 'yes'?" Jessica asked in a small voice.

Elizabeth sighed. "*Yes*, I guess it means yes. But after tomorrow, I'm through."

"Ouch!" Ellen yelled.

"What's the matter?" Betsy asked.

"I hammered my thumb."

"Again? That's the third time."

"Maybe if you'd let me use the good hammer instead of this crummy old thing I wouldn't keep smacking myself."

"Why don't you just pay attention to what you're doing and quit blaming everything on me?" Betsy retorted.

Elizabeth sighed. Kala's visit yesterday had

thrown everything off somehow. The work was going slowly, and the Unicorns had been squabbling all afternoon.

"Ouch!"

Elizabeth was getting tired of hearing that. Somebody seemed to be yelling about something every five minutes.

"Quit arguing and get to work," Janet commanded. She picked up a large beam, balanced it on her shoulder, and began stomping toward the shack with Betsy Gordon trailing a few feet behind her.

"Does she know what she's doing?" Elizabeth asked Mandy, who was standing nearby.

"Janet! Hold it!" Lila called out suddenly.

"What?" Janet yelled.

As she turned, the long end of the beam came around, hitting Betsy on the head.

"Ouch!" Betsy protested.

Mandy turned to Elizabeth. "I'd have to say that no, Janet doesn't know what she's doing. But I guess it doesn't matter. It's not like we're building the Taj Mahal. It doesn't have to last a thousand years—just until Halloween night."

"I can't imagine what kind of gross stuff we'd have to use to make this place last forever," Ellen interrupted loudly. "All this sealant is bad enough. It's all over my hands. Yuck!"

"Wash your hands in the creek," Elizabeth suggested. "The water is clear."

Ellen brightened at the thought. "Good idea." She dusted her hands on the seat of her jeans and hurried down toward the creek.

Elizabeth squatted down and began putting her tools away. It would feel good to rinse her own hot face in the creek. Out of the corner of her eye, she watched Ellen as she knelt down, bent over the water, and then recoiled in horror. "Oh, my gosh!" Ellen screamed.

"What is it?" Elizabeth jumped to her feet. Even after all Ellen's false alarms, she somehow sensed that the danger was real this time.

As Elizabeth ran to the creek, Mandy following behind her, Ellen half fell, half lurched backward up the bank. It took her only a few seconds to reach the top of the bank before she collapsed.

Elizabeth and Mandy hoisted her to her feet. "What is it?" Janet demanded. "What's wrong?"

Janet and Lila hurried over to join them.

Ellen's face was dead white. Even the color of her lips was gone. And she was trembling from head to foot.

"What is it, Ellen?" Janet demanded, shaking her.

Ellen's mouth opened, as if she were trying to speak, but nothing came out. Then she gave up and shuddered.

"Let her sit down," Tamara suggested softly.

Elizabeth and Mandy helped Ellen over to a flat rock. They sat her down and waited until some of the color began to return to her face.

"Ellen?" Mandy asked gently. "What happened? What scared you?"

"A skull," Ellen whispered. "A human skull."

"What?" Janet said with a gasp.

"When I bent my face over the creek, I saw it looking up at me from the bottom," she answered in a monotone.

"Probably just some kind of reflection from the sun," Grace said dismissively.

"No," Ellen insisted. "It wasn't. I saw what I saw."

"Ellen," Janet said in an impatient voice. "How many times have we heard this kind of thing from you? First, it's a bear, and now it's a skull. You probably saw a rock or something. Don't get so bent out of shape."

"I'm going to check this out myself," Elizabeth told Mandy softly.

She walked down the rocky bank that led to the creek, being careful not to trip or fall over any of the jagged stones.

When she reached the rock on which Ellen had balanced herself, she got down on her hands and knees and leaned over, looking down into the depths of the creek.

Suddenly, the earth seemed to tilt. Her balance was gone, and she could feel herself falling forward toward the shimmering surface of the water. *It can't be,* her mind was insisting as the black closed in around her. *It can't be.*

"Elizabeth!" she heard Mandy cry behind her.

A hand closed over the back of her shirt and yanked hard. Elizabeth tumbled back onto the rocks and fell against Mandy.

Mandy helped her to sit up on her own and then reached down and scooped up some of the cool water. "What's the matter?" she asked as she pressed her cool wet hands against Elizabeth's forehead and neck.

Gradually, Elizabeth regained her breath. "I'm OK," she said shakily. "It was just such a big shock."

"What was such a big shock?"

"Hold on to my feet," Elizabeth instructed.

As Mandy held her feet, Elizabeth lay on her stomach and reached her hand down into the water. When she found what she had been looking for, she hoisted it up toward the surface.

It was a skull—a cracked human skull yellowed with age.

As soon as the Unicorns saw it they began to scream.

"The boys put it there!" Janet shouted in an outraged tone. "I just know it!"

Elizabeth shook her head. "They couldn't have."

"How come?

"Because the garbage workers reported what happened to Mr. Clark. Mr. Clark assigned Jake and Rick and Bruce to ride around with the men and help every afternoon from now until Halloween. That way they can't get into any trouble."

"Then they must have come by last night after work," Janet insisted. "That's definitely what happened." She clapped her hands. "OK, everybody. Show's over. Let's get back to work."

The girls began to break up and drift back to the shack.

Everybody but Elizabeth. She sat on the bank and stared at the skull. *Who are you?* she asked silently. *How did you get here?*

But the skull just stared back at her with two dark, empty eye sockets.

"Hello, this is Elizabeth Wakefield. Is Jack back from his trip yet?" Elizabeth was calling the Houses for the Homeless office from a phone booth on her way home from Sleepy Hollow Road. If Jack was back, she was planning to ride over to his office and talk to him.

"I'm sorry," Beverly said. "He's not back yet, and I don't have a number where he can be reached. Is there anything you want me to tell him if he calls in?"

"Just ask him to call me," Elizabeth said. "No matter what time it is."

"Is it something important?" Beverly asked.

"I don't know," Elizabeth replied. "That's what I want him to tell me."

"Hello, this is Elizabeth Wakefield. May I speak to Kala, please?" Elizabeth looked at the grandfather

clock that stood in the front hall of the Wakefield house. It was nine o'clock. She was worried that it was a little late to be calling, but she knew that Kala was upset, and she wanted to fill her in on what had happened. "If she's asleep I can talk to her tomorrow at school."

"Kala isn't feeling well. And I don't think she'll be at school tomorrow," Kala's mother replied.

"Oh, I'm sorry to hear that. Will you tell her I called?" Elizabeth asked.

"I sure will, Elizabeth," Kala's mom promised.

Elizabeth hung up the phone and tightened the belt on her robe. She repeated Kala's words to herself: *The wolf told me.*

An eerie feeling stole over Elizabeth. She felt as if she were being watched—observed from the dark shadows of the living room.

Shivering slightly, she turned and ran up the stairs to her room, anxious to be within shouting distance of her parents and Jessica.

Eleven

◇

"The place is so creepy, I think we'll have to make a rule that nobody can leave our party and wander off," Jessica said on Monday morning. Several of the Unicorns were gathered at her locker when Rick Hunter, Bruce Patman, and Jake Hamilton had come over to ask about the skull.

Rumors about the Sleepy Hollow skull were already flying all over school. Some people had heard that the girls had found a skeleton. Some people had heard that they had found a whole body—mummified. And some people had heard that they had found several bodies scattered in the woods.

Jessica was bummed that she hadn't been there when they found the skull. But whether she was there or not, she still thought she was entitled to milk some publicity out of it.

Rick Hunter's eyes were wide with fascinated horror, and Bruce Patman peered at her intently. "You're sure it's a human skull? Some animal skulls look human, you know," Bruce pressed.

"It's a human skull, all right," Jessica replied confidently, thrilled with all the attention she was getting.

"How long do you think it had been down there?" Rick asked.

"Centuries maybe," Jessica answered.

Randy Mason had wandered over, and was listening from the edge of the group. "That is so unbelievably macabre," he said.

"What did he say?" Rick Hunter asked in an undertone.

"Creepy. Strange," Lila explained. "That's what *macabre* means."

Randy removed his glasses and wiped them with his handkerchief. "It's really macabre when you think about what those boys saw a couple of years ago. Remember? The group of skeletons walking up the road? They said one of them didn't have a head."

Jessica widened her eyes for maximum drama. "Don't you think it's possible that the person whose head it is might come to look for it on Halloween night?"

The boys' wide eyes grew even wider than Jessica's.

"It does . . . well . . . seem like the logical time," Rick said, clearing his throat.

"Wow. This whole thing is, like, so cool," Randy said.

"Well, all I know is I'm going to be there on Halloween night," Rick said. "If anything weird happens, I want to see it with my own eyes."

"Me, too," Bruce added. "Come on, Randy. Let's go to the lab and rig you up a mad-scientist costume."

"I'd rather go as the Monster from the Sweet Valley Lagoon," Randy said.

"What about going as the ghost of Elvis?" Bruce suggested.

As the boys disappeared down the hall, the girls let out a volley of controlled squeals.

"This party is going to be unforgettable!" Tamara said, happily clutching her books to her chest. "Everybody is going to be really, really spooked."

"Everybody including us," Mandy said with a shiver.

"How perfect is it that the Skeletons are going to be playing at this party?" Kimberly said excitedly.

There was another volley of shrieks from the group.

"Think we did the right thing with that skull?" Mary asked.

"Sure," Lila said. "What better thing to do with a skull than hang it on a nail in a tree? If somebody comes looking for it, they'll be sure to find it."

Jessica felt a sudden shiver. *Wow!* she thought. *Even I'm spooked. Hope I'll have the nerve to go to my own party.*

She closed her locker and hurried down the hall. Kala wasn't in school today, and Jessica decided that was just as well. If Kala was around, all the boys would be asking *her* for information instead of the Unicorns.

And thankfully the Unicorns were so distracted by the boys they hadn't pressed her for any more details about the Skeletons.

Jessica nervously bit her lower lip. So far, she'd had no luck cornering Scott. She had waited outside his house for hours yesterday hoping Steven and Joe would leave so that she could speak with him privately. But none of the boys came out of the house. It wasn't fair! Steven and Joe had hung out with Scott practically two whole days in a row, and Jessica hadn't gotten to talk to him for one second.

Fortunately, both Steven and Joe had basketball practice that afternoon. *Hopefully I'll get to talk to Scott and book the Skeletons for real.*

She didn't even want to think about what would happen if Scott said no.

". . . and after today I'm really through," Elizabeth insisted. It was Monday afternoon, and the girls were standing across the street from the music store, waiting for Scott to come out. They both held up large sections of the newspaper to hide their faces. "I'm sick and tired of playing cloak and dagger with Scott Timmons and . . ."

"Shhhh," Jessica warned.

"Jessica! Have you been listening to one word I said?"

"Sure, sure," Jessica said in a distracted voice as she peered across the street. "You're tired of breaking up fights between the Unicorns. You're ready to get back to your own life. And if I don't wrap this thing up today, you're *really* through." She grinned at Elizabeth. "Did I leave anything out?"

Elizabeth sighed. "No, that about covers it. But just for my information, what are you going to do if he says no?"

Jessica frowned. "I guess I'll have to move to another state and change my name. The Unicorns would probably be pretty mad at me and want revenge. Maybe I'd be eligible for the witness-protection program."

Elizabeth laughed. When Jessica had her mind made up about something, no setback could discourage her. She always had another half-baked plan or two up her sleeve. And she always managed to sucker Elizabeth into helping her, which was why Elizabeth was assisting in this stakeout.

"Here, hold my paper," Jessica instructed. Elizabeth took the paper from her, and Jessica opened her backpack and took out a compact. She studied her reflection in the tiny mirror. "Hmmmm. I wish I had put on more eye makeup."

"Are you kidding?" Elizabeth exclaimed. "You already look like the Bride of Frankenstein."

"Lizzie," Jessica said with a sigh, "you just don't understand show biz."

"Oh my gosh, there he is," Elizabeth whispered.

"Oh, nooo!" Jessica wailed. "He's with Steven. What's Steven doing here? He's supposed to have basketball practice."

"I guess they canceled it. Listen, Jess, I don't think you can wait any longer. Go and talk to Scott. Maybe it's better to have Steven there. It gives you a perfect excuse to walk up and start a conversation."

"Are you kidding? You know how Steven is when he's around other guys."

Elizabeth had to admit that Jessica was right. Steven couldn't help showing off by treating his sisters like little kids. "OK," she said as an idea clicked into place. "Leave it to me."

Elizabeth ran across the street and positioned herself in the front entrance of the grocery store. Just as Steven and Scott walked by, Elizabeth stepped out, almost bumping into them. "Steven! Boy, am I glad to see you."

"What's up, Elizabeth?" he asked.

"I promised Mom I'd get a bag of charcoal for cooking outside tonight. But all they have are the huge bags. I can't carry it by myself."

"Why can't you ask them to deliver it?"

Hmmm. Why *couldn't* Elizabeth ask them to deliver it? "The delivery boy is out sick today," she blurted in a burst of inspiration.

"Then go ahead and pay for it, and tell them that

Dad will come in the car tonight and pick it up."

"Dad's coming home late tonight," Elizabeth said promptly.

"*I'll* come back tonight, then," Steven said.

Elizabeth balled her fists in frustration as Steven and Scott continued on down the street. She had to do something, and she had to do something fast. "Ouch!" she screeched.

When Steven turned around to see what she was yelling about, she began hopping on one foot and holding the other foot in her hand.

"What's the matter?" Steven asked, hurrying over to her side.

"I have a cramp," Elizabeth moaned. "A terrible cramp."

"From what?"

"I don't know," Elizabeth wailed.

"How did you get here?" Scott asked.

"I walked," Elizabeth answered. Then she hopped up and down. "Ouch! Ouch!"

"Do you want to ride my bike home?" Steven asked.

Elizabeth shook her head. "I don't think I can pedal."

"That sounds like a pretty weird cramp," Steven said suspiciously.

"It's a *horrible* cramp," Elizabeth told him dramatically.

Steven folded his arms. "Since when do you get horrible cramps in your feet?"

"Well, geez, Steven," Elizabeth said, rolling her eyes. "There's a first time for everything. Ouch!"

Steven studied her for a few seconds.

"Ouch! Ouch!" she cried, leaning against the music store window.

Now Steven looked concerned. "I'll call Mom and ask her to come get you."

"Mom's not home," Elizabeth told him.

"I thought you said she sent you to get a bag of charcoal."

Since when was Steven such a stickler for detail? She couldn't think of anything to say, so she just squinched up her face as if she were in terrible pain. "Ouuuuch!"

"Never mind," Steven said quickly, hurrying toward the bike rack. "I'll pedal, and you can ride on the handlebars."

"I think that's the best thing," Elizabeth groaned.

"I'm sorry you're having such a rough time," Scott said kindly. "Maybe you should soak in a hot bathtub when you get home."

What I should do is soak my head for letting Jessica talk me into acting like an idiot, she thought miserably.

Steven held the bike and Scott helped her balance on the handlebars. "'Bye!" he called out.

"'Bye!" Elizabeth answered. As Steven turned the corner, she caught a glimpse of Jessica running out into the street.

Elizabeth steadied herself on the bars. Steven would probably catch on to her when he found out that Mrs. Wakefield had not, after all, asked Elizabeth to bring home a bag of charcoal.

But she would rather face an indignant Steven than a desperate Jessica. If Jessica couldn't pin Scott down today, there was no telling what kind of crazy scheme she might think up next.

Jessica hurried out from her hiding place as soon as Steven and Elizabeth had rounded the corner. She swiftly caught up with Scott and tapped him on the shoulder.

Scott turned and stared at her wide-eyed. "Elizabeth! How did . . . ?" Then his face broke into a grin. "Jessica!"

"Sorry I scared you." She smiled brightly. "Gosh, I guess *everybody's* jumpy these days. Even cool musician types."

Scott looked at her quizzically. "What's that supposed to mean?"

"Didn't you hear about the skull we found in the Sleepy Hollow creek?" she asked.

Scott shook his head. "No. I haven't heard anything about that."

Jessica quickly filled him in about the shack, the skull, the headless skeleton, and all the other creepy things that been happening to them.

"Wow. Real skulls and everything. Sounds like an awesome place for a Halloween party."

"I was hoping you would say that. What time can you be there?"

"Are you asking me for a date?" he teased.

"Yes and no," Jessica responded with a giggle. "I'm asking you and the rest of the Skeletons to play for our party on Halloween night. I mean, we have rumors of real skeletons and everything. What could be more perfect?"

Scott raised his eyebrows and laughed. "Are you sure you're only thirteen? You sure do maneuver like somebody older."

No, I'm only twelve, but there's no reason I have to remind you of that, Jessica thought with a smile.

"Please say yes," she said. "It'll be so much fun. And it's going to be such a cool party. We're calling it the Monster Ball."

"I don't know . . ." Scott mused. "It might not be safe." He cut his eyes right and left, as if he were afraid of being overheard. "Don't tell anybody this," he whispered, "but none of the guys in my band are very brave."

Jessica tossed her hair off her shoulders. "It's safe all right."

"Really? I thought you were expecting a headless skeleton. A *real* headless skeleton," he added. "That's what makes the party sound so cool."

Jessica's heart began to sink a little. Scott was nice, but he wasn't taking her seriously at all. He was teasing her. And it was clear he thought she couldn't win his game.

If she said the place wasn't haunted, he would say it wasn't a cool enough place to have a party. On the other hand, if she insisted that it was haunted, he would pretend to be too scared to go—*and* he would probably think she was a silly little kid.

Jessica racked her brain for something clever to say. *I need to trap him in his own net.* "If I'm not afraid to go there, then I don't see why a big guy like you should be afraid to go there," she said triumphantly.

Scott laughed and held up his hands. "OK, I'll make a deal with you. We'll do it just like in the monster movies."

"What are you talking about?" Jessica grinned, starting to feel more confident.

"My band will play your party on two conditions."

"What?"

"You spend an entire night at the Sleepy Hollow Road shack this Friday night. After all, we're musicians, not exorcists. If it's not safe, we want you to chase the ghosts out before we get there."

"What?" Her heart sank a little. Was he just trying to find a way out of playing the party? He was probably banking on her refusal to spend the night out there by herself.

Although he didn't actually say I had to be alone, she thought suddenly.

"OK," she agreed happily.

"OK?" he repeated.

Jessica laughed, enjoying how surprised he

looked. "So what's the second condition," she asked.

"You sing a song with my band on the night of the party."

Jessica's heart turned over. He had actually asked her to sing with him! "You're on."

Twelve

◇

Two hours later, Jessica stood in the doorway of Elizabeth's room, reading a list. "Janet Howell. Check. Betsy Gordon. Check. Ellen Riteman. Check. Lila Fowler. Check. Mary Wallace. Check. Kimberly Haver. Check. Tamara Chase. Check. Mandy Miller. Check." She grinned. "How did you do?"

Elizabeth turned from her desk to see Jessica practically dancing in her doorway. "I have to say, I think it's kind of weird that you're so excited about spending the night in a haunted house."

"Why is it weird? All the Unicorns, not to mention my dear sensible sister, will be there. It'll be a blast," Jessica said.

Elizabeth knew perfectly well that the real reason Jessica was so thrilled about spending the night at Sleepy Hollow Road had nothing to do with the slumber party itself. It had everything to do with Scott Timmons. Jessica would probably face down a hundred ghosts if it meant the chance to sing with Scott in front of all her friends.

"Elizabeth!" Jessica said impatiently. "Don't just sit there staring at me like I'm crazy. Who did you round up?"

Elizabeth put her pencil in her textbook to hold her place. "Amy's up for it and so is Maria."

"What did you tell them?"

"Just what you told me to say. That we really worked hard to clean the place up. And that we've got to make the most of the short time we have to enjoy it."

"Perfect," Jessica said happily. "What about Kala? Did you ask her?"

"I called her," Elizabeth said. "But her mom said she was still sick and would probably be out the rest of the week. I told her mom about the party and said that we wanted Kala to come if she felt like it. But I'm pretty sure she won't. I think she's had enough of Sleepy Hollow Road. *And* enough of us."

The phone rang, and Elizabeth started to get up. Maybe it was Jack Whitefeather.

But Jessica was already on her way. "I'll bet that's Belinda," she said as she ran down the stairs.

"Jessica!" Elizabeth heard her mother call from the kitchen. "Coming!" Jessica shouted back.

Elizabeth sighed, wondering where Jack was.

She put her hand in the pocket of her jeans and felt the stone arrowhead and the tooth that she had carried with her for the last few days.

Suddenly, her mouth felt dry, and she swallowed hard. She wasn't looking forward to the slumber party. She wasn't looking forward to it at all.

"What, exactly, is it that we're looking for?" Amy asked. It was late Friday afternoon and Elizabeth had coaxed Amy and Maria into coming early to Sleepy Hollow Road to keep her company.

"I'm not sure," Elizabeth answered.

"Is it bigger than a bread box?" Maria joked.

"I'm not sure," Elizabeth answered again in a serious tone.

It had been an incredibly busy week. Two tests. Three book reports. And an open-book quiz. Elizabeth had had no time to come out and look around on her own.

"I feel like an archaeologist," Amy said. "Oops. I think I just found another one."

Amy leaned over, scooped up the rudely crafted arrowhead, and put it with the small pile they had collected.

Elizabeth shook her head in amazement. "I can't believe we're finding all these arrowheads. I wonder what it means."

Amy shrugged. "It means that some Indians were here a long time ago. But finding arrowheads isn't that big a deal. People find arrowheads all over the place."

"I know, but . . ."

"But what?" Maria prompted.

"I think it does mean something else," Elizabeth said.

"Like what?" Amy and Maria asked at the same time.

She really didn't have any idea. But for some reason, she felt as if the answer was in the ground below. She took her spade and gently prodded the earth. "I just don't know."

As if on cue, her spade made a clinking noise. She had touched something hard. Maybe it was a rock. Elizabeth had leaned down to dig with her fingers when she heard someone hailing her from the road.

She looked up and saw Jessica arriving on her bike. Behind her were the rest of the Unicorns.

"We brought hot dogs and marshmallows!" Jessica shouted as they parked their bicycles.

Grace Oliver struggled out of her bulky backpack. "Sodas, too."

"Cool!" Maria said. "My stomach has been growling for the last half hour."

"Mine, too," Amy said. "Come on. Let's help them unload the supplies."

Elizabeth put her spade down and hurried to help so they could make camp before dark.

*   *   *

"Look at that moon," Jessica said, staring up at the sky.

Elizabeth felt strangely cold at the sight of the perfect full moon. Normally, she would have loved seeing that moon up there. But tonight it seemed spooky.

A lacy bit of dark cloud floated overhead, making shadow pictures against the glow of the moon. Elizabeth huddled closer to the blazing fire the girls had kindled outside the shack. She tried not to think of all the strange shapes she was seeing in the clouds when she looked up for a long time. The shape of a bear. The shape of a bat. The . . .

"Want another toasted marshmallow?" Amy asked her, interrupting her thoughts.

"Sure," Elizabeth said, glad for something as innocent as marshmallows to focus on. Listening to the scattered giggling and conversations around the campfire brought her mind back to the real world. *It's a good thing Kala isn't here*, she thought. *If she were, I'd never get my imagination under control.*

"Well," Jessica chirped, "so far so good. Nothing's come out of the woods yet to kill us."

"They're just waiting for us to finish eating," Maria joked. "They want us to fatten up first, like Hansel and Gretel."

Maria's joke provoked a lot of nervous giggles.

"You couldn't pay me a million dollars to take a walk through those woods at night," Janet

Howell said, casting a nervous glance toward the dark trees.

"Even with Denny Jacobson?" Grace Oliver teased.

The girls giggled even more.

Elizabeth drew a little bit closer to her sister. There was something reassuring about Jessica's laughing, giggling presence.

The fire fizzed and spat a little.

"It's going to be out soon," Amy commented. "Want me to throw a couple of logs on it?"

"Nah," Mandy Miller answered. "We'll be going inside soon to sleep. We might as well let it go out. It will save us the trouble of having to put it out with sand and dirt."

"Let's tell ghost stories," Maria suggested.

"Yes!" Kimberly and Mary shouted.

"No!" Mandy and Elizabeth shouted back.

"Oh, come on," Betsy said. "It'll be fun."

"Fun to scare ourselves silly?" Mandy argued. "No way. We'll just wind up getting so terrified we'll go home, and then everybody will laugh at us."

"Come on, Mandy," Lila said, "where's your sense of adventure?"

"No ghost stories," Janet Howell pronounced, rising from the ground. "Let's have another séance."

"Since we don't have a table," Janet instructed, "everyone hold hands."

All the girls were gathered inside the shack.

They sat in a circle on the floor around a single flickering candle.

Elizabeth felt Amy take her right hand and Maria take her left.

"Your hand is cold," Amy whispered in surprise. "You're not really scared, are you?"

"I just can't help feeling like this isn't a good idea," Elizabeth whispered back.

"We don't have to do this," Amy said softly.

"Everyone be quiet," Janet commanded. Then she closed her eyes and began swaying back and forth. "Concentrate," she commanded. "Close your eyes and concentrate."

Elizabeth closed her eyes and ordered herself to be calm and just have fun. There was probably nothing to this séance stuff anyway. It was just a silly game.

"Concentrate on the spirit world," Janet intoned.

Despite herself, Elizabeth furrowed her brow as she focused on spirits and ghosts and the shapes she had seen float past the moon.

"Ohhhh, spirit world," Janet brayed in a pleading voice. "Join us."

Elizabeth half expected to hear Jessica clowning around in some way—making a ghostly moan or something.

"Spirit world," Janet moaned, "do you hear us?"

Elizabeth wished that Jessica would hurry up and start faking it. There was too much tension in the air. She was ready for some comic relief.

But only Janet's occasional plea to the spirits broke the deep silence.

Elizabeth tried to force the muscles in her neck to relax. Nothing real or unreal was going to happen—not to a bunch of ordinary middle-school girls sitting around a candle and . . .

Blam! The door of the shack burst open and banged against the wall.

Grace Oliver let out a high-pitched scream, and Ellen began to shriek, as a howling, hurtling wind swept into the room. The candle blew out and the room was suddenly dark.

"What is it?" Tamara wailed.

"Who is it?" Lila screamed.

"Where is it?" Mandy shouted.

A gust of wind blew past Elizabeth's ear. *"Believe,"* a soft voice whispered. She jumped at the sound.

Who had said that? Who had been close enough to her to whisper right in her ear?

A beam of moonlight came streaming through the window, and Elizabeth saw Maria struggling to close the door. "It's just the wind," she shouted. "Everybody get a grip."

Maria pushed the door against the gust, banging it shut. The howling sound came to a stop. "There," Maria said in a satisfied voice. "No more spirits."

Everybody laughed nervously, breaking the terrible grip of fear in the room.

Janet struck a match and relit the candle. "Did

anybody feel or see anything strange?" she asked.

They all shook their heads.

"Well," she said impatiently, "since you people are obviously not capable of the level of concentration needed to reach the spirit world, we might as well try to get some sleep."

"Where do you want to put our sleeping bags?" Amy asked Elizabeth as the girls reached for their belongings.

Elizabeth took some deep breaths, trying to calm her racing heart. "As far from the door as possible," she answered.

Blam!

Elizabeth woke from a deep sleep, looked toward the door, and then sat straight up and screamed.

"Ahhhhhhhhh!"

A cloaked figure stood in the doorway, silhouetted against the moon.

Elizabeth's scream woke the rest of the girls. They all began shrieking at the sight of the figure.

"Who is it?" someone's sleepy voice wailed from a dark corner. "Who's there?"

"Where's my flashlight?" Elizabeth heard Amy mutter.

After what seemed like an hour, Amy located her flashlight and shone it toward the door.

"Kala!" the entire group exclaimed.

Kala stood in the doorway wearing a woven wool poncho.

"I thought you didn't want to come," Elizabeth said in a trembling voice. She tried to stand, but her legs were shaking, and they were so wobbly, they couldn't support her.

Amy's flashlight beam illuminated Kala's face. Her eyes looked empty, and her face was expressionless.

"Why don't you come in, Kala," Elizabeth asked weakly. "You must be cold out there."

But Kala made no move to step into the shack. "I have another message," she said in a flat tone. "From the old ones."

"What?" Janet asked irritably. "What were you doing over at their house at this time of night?"

"Stop the construction," Kala said. "Stop the construction or the old ones will be very angry."

"I told you before," Lila began. "Those old people . . ." She broke off as Kala backed out of the doorway and disappeared into the shadows.

Amy and Maria jumped up and went to the door.

"Kala!" Maria called out. "Come back and spend the night. It's too late to be out by yourself."

"Kala!" Amy echoed. "Come back."

But there was no answering voice from outside.

"Oh, for goodness' sake," Maria said as she shut the door. "Kala is as bad as you are, Jessica."

"What does that mean?" Jessica demanded in a hurt voice.

Maria looked at her watch. "Jokes at two o'clock in the morning. Please! Aren't we a little old for this stuff? Somebody needs to have a serious talk with that girl tomorrow."

Elizabeth's heart was still pounding in her rib cage. Something was wrong, but she didn't know what. All she knew was that somewhere, out there in the dark night, strange forces were at work. "Let's leave," she said suddenly.

"What?" Lila cried.

"Let's leave," Elizabeth repeated. "I think we should leave."

"I wouldn't mind leaving, either," Grace said.

"Neither would I," Ellen said, looking around the room. "I've had enough scares for one night."

Jessica stood up and threw her sister an angry look. "Come on, you guys. If we don't stay overnight, everybody will say we were chicken."

And more important, the Skeletons won't play at your party, Elizabeth thought sourly.

"She's right," Janet said. "She's absolutely right. As an eighth grader and president of the Unicorns, I absolutely forbid anyone to leave."

"What do you want to do, Elizabeth?" Amy said softly. "If you want to leave, we'll ride home with you." She turned to Maria. "Right?"

"Right," Maria echoed. She reached over and squeezed Elizabeth's shoulder.

Maria's warm hand felt strong and reassuring. So did Amy's practical, no-nonsense attitude.

"Let's stay," Elizabeth said. "I was just being silly. I guess I sort of lost my head."

"You and the rest of us." Mandy laughed. "Betsy jumped ten feet and landed right on top of me."

Everybody began to giggle.

"Good thing Betsy didn't have too many marsh-mallows," Grace joked.

While everyone resettled their sleeping bags, Amy turned her flashlight off and lay back down.

Elizabeth waited for her eyes to adjust to the dark. Before long she could make out the shapes and silhouettes of all the girls surrounding her.

She turned over on her side so she could watch the door.

She had no intention of going back to sleep. If there were any more nighttime visitors, she wanted to be ready to run.

Thirteen

◇

"Brrrrrr!" Maria shivered as she sat up.

The first sunlight was streaming in through the window, waking the girls and illuminating the inside of the shack.

Elizabeth had stayed awake all night going over and over the events of the past few days. Of course, there could be rational explanations for most of them. Someone could be playing a joke, an intricately plotted prank.

But somehow even that didn't make much sense. No one could have planned and executed all the strange things that had happened without Kala's full cooperation.

Could Kala have been pretending? Was she in league with Rick? Or Bruce? Or Jake?

Was she in league with Jessica?

Elizabeth remembered the purple circles under Kala's eyes and the unhappy, confused expression on her face. She hadn't known Kala long, so she had nothing to go on except her own instincts. And her instincts told her to trust Kala.

"Ready to go home?" Jessica asked, hoisting her sleeping bag over her shoulder.

"I'm going to make a stop first," Elizabeth said.

"Well, count me out of your stop," Jessica said, straightening out her rumpled T-shirt. "I've got a very important phone call to make." She grinned. "And then I'm going to practice my singing. *Get ready for the monster ball. It's the spookiest party of all.*" She shimmied her shoulders as she sang.

"I'm ready for some breakfast," Grace said, sitting up and stretching.

"I'm ready for a hot shower," Mandy said through a yawn, pushing her tousled hair out of her eyes.

"I'm ready for some Saturday-morning tube," Ellen put in.

I'm ready to get out of here, Elizabeth thought, jumping up and pulling on her jeans.

"So you *do* believe me?" Kala asked.

Elizabeth had stopped by Kala's house on the way home from the shack, and they were sitting in Kala's bedroom.

Elizabeth nodded. "I'm not sure exactly what it is that we're both believing. But I think we should start trusting our instincts—and trusting each other."

Kala smiled. "It's a deal. I'd light up the peace pipe, but I don't smoke."

Elizabeth giggled and looked around Kala's bedroom. Every shelf was covered with Native American artifacts. Framed pieces of old cloth hung on the wall.

"Wow!" Elizabeth said. "It's like a Native American museum in here." She walked around the room touching some of the objects and taking in some of the atmosphere. Somewhere, there was a connection between Kala's interest in her Native American heritage and the strange images that came to her in her dreams. Somewhere, there was a link.

"Kala!" Kala's mother's voice called out. "Would Elizabeth like to stay for some pancakes?"

"You bet," Elizabeth answered. "Let's eat some ceremonial pancakes, and then plot our strategy."

"Is Jessica going to help us?" Kala asked.

Elizabeth smiled. "I think Jessica's going to be too busy thinking about the Monster Ball to be much help. If I know Jessica, she's probably speed-dialing Scott Timmons as we speak."

"Hello?"

"This is Jessica Wakefield, reporting alive from the Wakefield kitchen after spending the night on Sleepy Hollow Road." Jessica plopped down at the kitchen table and cradled the receiver between her shoulder and her ear.

"You really stayed the whole night?" Scott asked in a teasing voice. "You didn't chicken out and go home early, did you?"

Jessica curled up happily in her chair. Scott was so much fun to flirt with. "We didn't chicken out," she said in a cocky voice. "Now, let's see how brave the Skeletons are!"

Scott laughed. "We'll be there. But don't forget— you have to sing."

"There it is, " Elizabeth told Kala in a breathless voice. "See. There's a big FOWLER CONSTRUCTION sign." She pointed toward a huge warehouse building surrounded by men and utility vehicles.

It was Monday after school, and Elizabeth was sweating and a little out of breath after the long, mostly uphill ride out to Fowler Construction.

The girls turned up the gravel driveway, pedaling until they reached the fence that surrounded the yard.

Men and women streamed in and out of an enormous warehouse with beams of lumber and steel balanced on their shoulders. Other workers were pushing wheelbarrows full of bricks and building materials.

Two men pounded rocks into gravel with their jackhammers and several trucks were backed up and parked for loading. The roar of the truck engines combined with the clatter of the jackhammers made a deafening noise.

Elizabeth and Kala got off their bicycles, leaned them against the chain-link fence, and walked into the yard.

They passed a man who smiled at the girls and moved his lips, but Elizabeth couldn't hear a thing.

She tugged slightly at Kala's sleeve, and the two of them walked over to see the man.

"Can . . . elp . . . ou" was all she was able to catch.

"We'd like to see the foreman," Elizabeth shouted.

The man held his hand up to his ear.

"We'd like to see the foreman!" Elizabeth shouted even louder.

The man nodded and pointed toward the inside of the building. He mouthed something that Elizabeth didn't catch, but she understood what he meant. She smiled her thanks and then led Kala through the jumble of trucks and materials into the warehouse.

Inside, she looked around and saw that the back of the warehouse was partitioned off with glass to form an office. She and Kala went to the door and knocked.

A secretary motioned them in, and Elizabeth and Kala stepped inside and closed the door behind them.

"WE WOULD LIKE TO SEE THE FOREMAN!" Elizabeth bellowed.

The secretary looked startled. "It's not necessary to shout."

Elizabeth closed her mouth in embarrassment. "Oh, sorry," she said in a more normal voice, noticing the heavy windows. "It was . . . um, really loud out there."

The secretary lowered her hands from her ears. "May I help you girls?"

"We'd like to see the foreman," Kala answered.

"Will he know what this is about?" she asked.

"We'd like to talk to him about the property on Sleepy Hollow Road," Elizabeth said.

The door to an office opened, and a familiar-looking man walked out. It was the same man who had come to Sleepy Hollow Road a few days before and told them about the construction. "Unicorns," he said, smiling as he recognized the girls.

Elizabeth smiled and shook her head. "Actually, no. The Unicorns are a club, and we're not members. But we are members of the group who worked to restore the shack and clean up the Sleepy Hollow property. That's what we wanted to talk to you about."

The man tucked his clipboard under his arm. "Doing an article in your little school paper about the new tower?" he asked with an indulgent smile. "That ought to make a good article. I think we could probably even arrange to get you girls some pictures. How would you like that? Hmmm?"

"We're not here about a school project,"

Elizabeth responded, trying to sound very grown up. "We're here about the development on Sleepy Hollow."

The man smiled. "What do you think all this activity is about? We're getting ready to break ground right after Halloween."

"But you can't!" Kala cried out.

The man looked at Kala, raising his eyebrows. "What's the matter? Are you worried about your clubhouse?" He gave her braid a friendly tug. "Don't you worry. Mr. Fowler already talked to some of the guys. We'll be out there with a flatbed to move the place before demolition starts."

"Move the place?" Elizabeth repeated in confusion.

The man stood and pulled on his suspenders. "After our conversation the other morning, I kind of got the impression that that clubhouse was important to you girls. So I told Mr. Fowler, and he told us that on the day after Halloween, we should plan on moving the shack to another piece of property nearer town. Ain't that great?"

"That's really nice," Elizabeth said. "The Nature Scouts will be happy to have a clubhouse. But actually, that's not what we're concerned about."

"No?"

Elizabeth and Kala shook their heads.

"We want to talk to you about the construction," Elizabeth explained.

"What about it?"

"It's got to be stopped."

"Stopped?" he asked in a tone of disbelief.

Elizabeth and Kala nodded.

The foreman took off his hard hat and scratched his head. Then he sighed heavily and replaced the hat. "Young ladies, do you two represent one of those no-growth organizations? Because if you do, I just want you to know that approximately two hundred and thirty men and women, their children, and their neighborhoods will receive benefits from the construction starting as of day one. This job is going to be a big employer, and these days, people need jobs more than they need vacant lots."

"That's not it," Elizabeth argued. "We know this project helps workers and improves the economy, but there's something strange about that property." She gestured to Kala. "Maybe you can explain."

Kala took a deep breath. "See, a couple of weeks ago, we had this séance—"

The foreman cut her off with a derisive snort and strode to the door. "Henry!" he yelled. "Come down here!" He motioned to a young man in the warehouse to come down from a ladder.

Henry quickly complied and came over to join the group. The foreman gave them a thin smile. "Henry, would you please show these two young ladies off of the property. And then put up the sign that says MEN AND WOMEN WORKING."

"Listen, if someone could just hear us out . . ." Elizabeth began as Henry gripped her arm, guiding her and Kala toward the front gate. "It would only take a few . . ."

Henry gave both girls a gentle push, sending them outside the gate, which he then shut with a loud bang.

Elizabeth stared helplessly at the FOWLER CONSTRUCTION sign.

"Now what?" Kala asked in a frustrated voice.

"I think we need to take this to the top," Elizabeth replied.

Fourteen

◇

"So you see," Kala said, winding up her long and involved story, "the old ones don't want you to construct the office building. At least that's what they told me."

The security guard who sat behind the desk in the lobby of Fowler Enterprises gazed at Kala with bored, heavy-lidded eyes. He drummed his fingers on the desk. "Anything else you want to tell me?" he asked, raising one brow.

"They'll be very angry if the construction isn't stopped," Kala added.

Elizabeth had the uncomfortable feeling that they weren't being very convincing. The bald facts sounded kind of silly. But she couldn't think of any better way to tell it.

The security guard pulled a pen from his pocket

and began to fiddle with it. "OK, let me see if I've got this right. You want to see Mr. Fowler about the Sleepy Hollow Tower. If he doesn't cancel the construction, some old folks—"

"Old *ones*," Kala corrected.

"Old *ones*," he amended, "are going to be very angry."

"That's right," Kala confirmed.

"And you know this because some animals told you in a dream."

Kala winced. "Um . . . yeah. More or less."

The security guard let out a long sigh. Then he reached for his radio. "This really isn't my department, girls, if you can hang on just a . . ."

The hand-held radio came to life with a loud rattle of static. "Bowers here," said a voice on the other end.

"Yeah, Bowers, this is the front desk and it's definitely trick-or-treat season. I've got a couple of W-E-I-R-D-O-S here and—"

"If that's supposed to be a code," Elizabeth said angrily, "that's pretty lame. We can spell, you know."

But before she could complain any further, she heard the sound of feet running up a stairwell. The exit door burst open, and two armed guards sprang into the lobby and began bearing down on them.

"Hey!" Elizabeth yelled. "Not so fast. We need to see Mr. Fowler."

"Mr. Fowler is a very busy man," one of the

guards said, taking her firmly by the shoulder.

"But he knows me," Elizabeth protested. "I go to school with his daughter."

Elizabeth felt the firm hand loosen its grip. "Really? What's her name?" He shot the question at Elizabeth as if he were trying to determine whether or not she was an enemy spy.

"Her name is Lila, and she's in the sixth grade, and she's also a member of the Unicorn Club."

"We both go to Sweet Valley Middle School with Lila," Kala added.

The uniformed guards exchanged a look, then let go of the girls' shoulders and stepped a few feet away. They held a whispered consultation with the man behind the desk and seemed to reach a decision.

The man behind the desk wrote them out a pass. "Take the second elevator on the left to the fifth floor and ask for Mrs. King."

Elizabeth and Kala looked toward the other guards for confirmation. Both guards touched the brims of their caps and gave them a respectful nod.

"Well," Elizabeth said to Kala as they got into the elevator and punched the button. "I guess this proves it's not what you know, it's who you know. Now maybe we'll get some action."

"How long have we been sitting here?" Kala asked.

Elizabeth looked at her watch. "Almost an hour," she answered drearily.

The girls were sitting in a little outer office lounge on the fifth floor. Two women and a man hurried past them heading toward the elevators. All three carried briefcases.

"I guess it's almost closing time," Kala whispered as another group of people came out of their offices and drifted toward the door.

The heavy oak doors that led to the inner offices opened, and a woman stepped into the lobby. "Mrs. King will see you now."

The girls got up and followed the woman through a long curving hallway. They stopped at a plush, sunny office at the end of the hall, where a woman sat behind a huge desk. She looked up with a big smile. "So you're friends of Lila's."

"Yes, ma'am, I'm . . ."

"You're Jessica, her best friend." Mrs. King smiled. "I met you one afternoon at the Fowlers' mansion." She smiled and gestured toward two chairs on the other side of her desk.

"Actually, I'm not Jessica," Elizabeth said quickly. "I'm Jessica's twin sister, Elizabeth. And this is my friend Kala. She goes to Sweet Valley Middle School with me and Jessica and Lila."

"I see," Mrs. King said, still smiling politely. "And what is this about?"

"It's about Sleepy Hollow Road. The office tower you're getting ready to build."

"Ahhhh. I understand now. Mr. Fowler informed me that you girls have a clubhouse or some such thing on that property. Well, it's a shame it has to be moved, but as chief architect at Fowler Enterprises, I think I can guarantee that we can find you a suitable piece of property to use as a substitute. And you don't have to worry about the loss of natural beauty. You have my word that every effort has been made to integrate the sur-- rounding woods and creek into the overall layout."

"It still has to be stopped," Kala insisted softly.

Mrs. King arched her eyebrows. "What are you talking about?"

Kala quickly recounted her dreams and the warning from the old ones.

"My dear," Mrs. King said huffily, "you can hardly expect me to cancel a multimillion-dollar construction project simply because you had one or two bad dreams."

"It's not just one or two bad dreams," Kala insisted. "I know it's hard to understand. I don't really understand it myself. But those dreams were warnings. If the construction isn't stopped, something bad will happen."

The phone on Mrs. King's desk rang and she reached for it. "Hello . . . yes . . . yes . . ." She looked at Kala and Elizabeth, then swiveled around in her chair so that her back was toward them. "That's right," she said, dropping her voice to a low whisper. "Two of Lila's schoolmates . . . playing a prank, I think."

Mrs. King swiveled around again to face the

girls. She widened her eyes in surprise. "Very well," she said in a clipped voice. "I'll send them right up."

Mrs. King replaced the receiver. "Mr. Fowler has been informed that you are here. He would like to see you in his office."

"Elizabeth! What a nice surprise." Mr. Fowler was waiting for them when they stepped out of the elevator.

Elizabeth smiled back and shook Mr. Fowler's hand. "This is my friend Kala. Kala, this is Mr. Fowler."

"How do you do," Mr. Fowler said, smiling at Kala before turning back to Elizabeth. "Mrs. King seems to think you girls want to stop the Sleepy Hollow Tower construction. I think I understand how you feel. You've worked hard to clean it up, and now you feel attached to the place. But I want you to see something."

He led the girls down the corridor and into a conference room. Sitting on the big oval table was a miniature replica of two sleek and beautiful office buildings with lots and lots of windows. To one side lay the woods, and on the other side ran the creek. A tiny billboard read *Sleepy Hollow Tower A.*

"You see? The property isn't spoiled at all. We've preserved most of the wooded area and put picnic tables in the shady spots so that workers can enjoy their lunches outside when the weather is nice."

Mr. Fowler's finger moved toward the creek. "We're adding aquifers every few miles to be sure we don't pollute the water during construction. When we get through, that water will be clean enough to drink." Mr. Fowler cast a proud glance over the model. "It's going to be beautiful. A real asset to the area."

"But you can't build it," Kala said quietly.

"Why on earth not?" Mr. Fowler demanded.

"I know this is weird," she repeated for the millionth time, "but the old ones will be angry."

Mr. Fowler threw back his head and roared with laughter. "If you're talking about the old couple next door, they're *thrilled* about it. In order to get enough land for the project, I had to buy them out. And I did—at ten times the market value of their land! They're a nice old couple, and now, because of this, they're going to have a very comfortable retirement in Palm Springs."

Elizabeth felt a flush of embarrassment. Mr. Fowler sounded perfectly reasonable, and nothing she and Kala had to say seemed very convincing.

Kala looked just as embarrassed as she stared at the floor.

"I'm sorry to bother you, Mr. Fowler," Elizabeth managed to mutter. "Thanks for your time." She steered Kala toward the door.

"Don't you worry," Mr. Fowler called out behind them. "We won't touch one thing until after your Halloween party."

They rode the elevator down in silence. Once they were outside and heading back to their bicycles, Kala let out a long, mournful sigh. "I must really sound completely loony, but I *know* my dreams are important. And I know they mean something. I just don't know what to do."

"I don't either," Elizabeth said softly. "But I think we'd better call it a day. It's almost dark."

As they reached their bicycles, Elizabeth heard a dog howling in the distance—a long, baying howl that sounded more like a wolf's.

Kala seemed lost in thought as she climbed on her bicycle. "I'll bet you think I'm kind of crazy, don't you?"

"No," Elizabeth protested, "I don't."

"Well, I feel kind of crazy," Kala said.

"Well, then we're crazy," Elizabeth reassured her.

"The people at school already think I'm a weirdo," Kala said unhappily. "When they hear about what happened today, they'll laugh their heads off."

"They won't know about today," Elizabeth pointed out.

Kala looked skeptical. "I'm sure Mr. Fowler will say something to Lila. And even if he doesn't, those construction men will probably tell the story all over Sweet Valley. I hope this doesn't make you a laughingstock. I mean, it doesn't matter so much about me. I'll be moving on in a couple of weeks. But you'll have to stay here."

Elizabeth smiled. "Don't worry. Believe me, if I can survive having Jessica as a sister, I can definitely survive having you as a friend. So," she added, trying to sound cheerful and positive, "are you ready for the Monster Ball tomorrow night?"

Kala shook her head. "I don't think so. And I don't think I'll be at school tomorrow, either. I'm really tired. I think I'm coming down with something. And I just—" Her voice broke slightly. "I just don't think I can face anyone."

Elizabeth reached over to touch Kala's hand on the handlebar, but Kala wouldn't meet her eyes. She stood up on her bike and quickly pedaled off into the twilight.

Elizabeth felt a cold, damp wind. She shivered and looked at her watch. There was still a little time before she had to get ready for dinner—and a little time before Houses for the Homeless closed up shop for the night. *Maybe Jack Whitefeather is back in town,* she thought hopefully. Maybe she'd finally be able to get ahold of him.

"Jack? No, he's not back yet, but we expect him any day now. Maybe even tomorrow. Go on in and leave a note," Beverly suggested once Elizabeth had reached the Houses for the Homeless site. She gestured toward the trailer that Jack used as a mobile office.

"Thanks," she said. "I think I will."

It was late and there weren't many people left at the site. Inside the trailer, there was a desk piled high with papers. Elizabeth scanned the overflowing bookshelf against the wall. The top shelf contained books on construction, novels, how-to books, and pamphlets. And on the middle shelf, there was a whole collection of books on Native Americans and their history.

Elizabeth wished Kala could have been there to see all of it. A sudden draft of cold air brushed past her cheek and ruffled the papers on Jack's desk. Elizabeth retrieved a loose page from the floor and placed it back on the desk next to a large, heavy reference book.

A second draft chilled the interior of the trailer and raised goose bumps along Elizabeth's arms.

Elizabeth jumped at the sudden thudding noise. The heavy front cover of the book on the desk had blown open. And the chilly breeze was riffling the pages like an invisible finger.

Finally, the invisible finger seemed to find its place, and the book rested open.

Slowly, with her heart pounding in her throat, Elizabeth looked down on the page. She gasped.

They were all there.

The bat.

The bear.

The eagle.

And the wolf.

They were painted on the border surrounding the base of a clay pot.

Elizabeth squinted, reading the small type of the caption underneath the photograph.

"A Native American burial pot," it read.

Fifteen

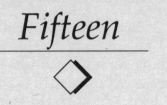

"Dad agreed to drive out and bring all the sodas and food and everything. And the Fowlers' chauffeur is going to rig up a generator for the band to use," Jessica told Elizabeth excitedly. "Mrs. Purvis said she'd chaperone."

It was Tuesday afternoon, and the last bell at Sweet Valley Middle School had just rung.

Jessica cast a pleased look about her. "Everybody is coming to the party," she said happily.

"Let me borrow your skeleton costume," Dennis Cookman was begging Rick Hunter as they hurried down the hall.

"No way," Rick replied. "Get your own costume. I'm going to need mine tonight."

"What are you going to wear?" Jessica asked Elizabeth.

"Oh," Elizabeth said, caught offguard. "I guess I forgot about a costume." She shrugged. "I don't know, I'll figure out something. Maybe Mom will let me have an old sheet. I can cut eyeholes and come as a ghost."

"Weak!" Jessica protested. "Can't you come up with a better idea than that? This is your chance to wear something fun and exciting, and you want to wear a sheet over your head?"

"I know, I know. I'll try to think of something better," Elizabeth promised, turning to leave.

"Where are you going?" Jessica asked.

"Out to Sleepy Hollow Road," she called back over her shoulder.

"But it's too early. There's nobody there."

Exactly, Elizabeth thought. She had a little private investigating to do.

Elizabeth poked around with the spade very gently. Was it here?

No.

Here maybe?

No.

There?

Clink!

Elizabeth put down her spade and dropped to her knees. She carefully dug into the dirt. It was only a few inches below the surface. And if it was what she thought it was, it was very fragile.

Finally, her hand closed over something hard. It

felt like clay. She lifted it from the dirt and stared at it in amazement. It was whole and perfectly smooth. It looked exactly like the one in Jack Whitefeather's book.

A Native American burial pot.

"Elizabeth!" Mrs. Purvis, the Fowlers' live-in housekeeper, exclaimed when she opened the imposing front door of the Fowlers' mansion. "What are you doing here? All the other girls are at your house getting ready for the party."

"I'm actually here to see Mr. Fowler," Elizabeth told her. "I called his office from a pay phone, but they said he had already left and gone home."

"I'm afraid you just missed him," Mrs. Purvis replied. "He just left to go to Los Angeles for a business meeting."

Elizabeth's heart sank. "And there's no way to reach him tonight?"

"Well," Mrs. Purvis looked at her watch. "I suppose you could try calling the car phone. But he's driving himself, and unless he's expecting something very important, he doesn't take calls. He doesn't like having to divert his attention from the road."

Elizabeth thought for a moment. Somehow, confronting Mr. Fowler while he dodged traffic on the freeways outside of Los Angeles didn't seem like the best idea. If anything, the phone call would only irritate him. *He'd probably think I was totally ridiculous,* she thought. *Even more ridiculous than he thought before.*

"More eye makeup," Mandy said decisively.

Lila picked up the makeup wand and put more dark shadow on her lid, making her eyes more cat-like.

"Lila!" Elizabeth said impatiently. "Are you listening?"

Before Lila could answer, Grace Oliver turned the volume on the Johnny Buck tape up to an ear-splitting level.

All the Unicorns were gathered in Jessica's room, getting ready for their party. Elizabeth had spent the last ten minutes trying to talk to Lila over the music and the girls' squealing about the party. But she seemed unable to make Lila pay attention.

There were clothes scattered over every inch of the floor. And every surface was littered with makeup, sequins, and glitter.

"Well?" Janet Howell said, spinning around to show off her costume. She was dressed as a dead rock star. Her face was made up to look ghostly white. She wore red bell-bottoms and a fringed leather vest from the sixties, and had her hair teased until it stood almost straight out.

"You look totally—dead," Tamara told her, slinking around in her black cat suit.

"Do you think I should fill up my oilcan some more?" Mandy asked, rapping on her costume with her fist. She was dressed as the Tin Man from *The Wizard of Oz.*

"I don't know, but I need someone to cut my wedding dress," Betsy Gordon said. "I can't reach the hem in back." She was the Bride of Frankenstein, dressed in a cheap wedding dress she'd found in a thrift shop.

"I'll do it," Mary Wallace offered. She took a pair of shears and began making big tears in Betsy's hem and sleeves. "Now could you help me pour this fake blood down my bodice?"

"Has anyone seen that silver eyeliner?" Lila asked.

"Lila!" Elizabeth tried again, raising her voice. "Are you listening?"

"I just saw that liner a second ago," Lila said, shaking out her Snow White wig.

"Ta-da!" Jessica announced from the bathroom doorway. She was dressed in Mrs. Wakefield's long black dress, and her hair was piled high on her head. She took Lila's hand, and the two of them began dancing to the music while the other girls screamed with laughter.

Elizabeth sighed. When the Unicorns were getting ready for a party—or any boy/girl event, for that matter—they were impossible to talk to. All they could do was squeal, giggle, and dance around.

"So where's your costume?" Tamara asked Elizabeth.

Elizabeth didn't bother to answer. She'd never make herself understood over all this noise, and Tamara was bopping around too excitedly to notice. Besides, Elizabeth really needed to let Kala know what was going on.

"A burial ground!" Kala exclaimed in shock.

Elizabeth nodded.

Kala stood up and began pacing her bedroom. "Now it's making sense. It's all making sense. I think I know what the dreams mean. I know who the *old ones* are. They're the people who were here before we were—the Native Americans. And I understand why they want the construction stopped. Burial grounds are sacred, and it's wrong to build things over a final resting place."

Kala stopped in midpace. "But what I don't understand is—*why me*? I mean, why did *I* have the dreams. Why did they send *me* the message. Why didn't they contact somebody like Mr. Fowler? He's the one who needs to be convinced."

"Maybe you had the dreams because you're part Native American," Elizabeth answered thoughtfully. "Maybe you're descended from some of the people buried on that property. That's why you were chosen as the medium—from the very first séance."

"Wow!" Kala exclaimed as everything seemed to sink in. "And in some crazy way, the skull makes sense, too. Probably some animals or machinery dug up some bones of people buried there." She looked at her hands. "And now it's pretty clear why my dreams were telling me to stop the construction—they'll be building over people's graves."

"Maybe they won't," Elizabeth said solemnly. "I called Houses for the Homeless. Jack Whitefeather will be back in town tomorrow. Maybe he'll believe us and help us convince Mr. Fowler."

Kala looked at her. "I really hope you're right."

"In the meantime," Elizabeth continued, standing up, "I think we ought to go to the party. We certainly earned it after all our hard work."

"I don't know, Elizabeth," Kala said softly.

"Don't worry, it won't be just the Unicorns. Amy will be there. And Maria. Practically all of the *Sixers* staff. And Jessica is sure that lots of other kids will come, since the Skeletons are going to play."

Kala bit her lip, thinking hard. "I don't think I'll go," she said firmly. "It might seem disrespectful of me."

Elizabeth smiled. "I think I understand. I hope you won't think it's disrespectful if I go."

"No, you should go," Kala assured her. "You'll probably want to keep an eye on Jessica."

"On Jessica?" Elizabeth asked with a laugh. "Why would I need to keep my eye on her?"

"Just in case there's any danger," Kala answered.

Sixteen

◇

"The Skeletons are really blown away to be here," Scott announced into the microphone over the clamor of the party. Jessica felt her stomach flutter as he smiled in her direction.

Everyone applauded wildly.

"Is everybody having a good time?" he shouted.

"Yeah!" the crowd answered in a roar.

Jessica stood up front, her heart racing. She looked around her excitedly. So far, this had been the absolute coolest, most incredible party anyone had ever seen. The shack was full of kids in costume, and some of the masks were so spooky and elaborate that Jessica couldn't tell who was behind them.

But best of all was the moment the Skeletons had shown up. Scott flirted with her as if she were

at least fourteen. He even put his arm around her
shoulders once while he was waiting for the other
members of the band to set up. The Unicorns were
totally awestruck when they saw this.

"Is everybody having fun?" Scott yelled again.

"Yeah!" the crowd shouted.

"Ready for something really special?" he asked.

The crowd roared its approval.

Jessica's heart did somersaults.

"Since we agreed to play here tonight," Scott
said, "Jessica Wakefield has agreed to sing a song
with us." The crowd erupted into applause, and
Scott held out his hand to Jessica.

She was so nervous her legs were shaking. But
there was no tremor in her voice. It came out loud
and strong as Scott hit the first chord and the two
of them launched into the first chorus of "The
Monster Ball."

"Jessica sounds great!" Amy exclaimed, wrap-
ping her vampire's cape around her.

"Doesn't she?" Elizabeth agreed proudly.

The Skeletons were terrific. And Jessica's voice
blended beautifully with Scott's.

"By the way," Amy added, "that's a great costume. Where did you get it?"

"Kala put it all together," Elizabeth answered.

Kala had thought of the idea just before
Elizabeth left for the party. She'd thought Elizabeth
could show the proper respect at the burial ground

by wearing traditional Native American garb to the party. Kala had lent her a beautifully beaded buckskin shift, some soft moccasins, and a woven blanket to protect her from the chill.

"Come on," Amy said. "Let's move a little closer."

The two girls shouldered their way through the crowd at the door of the shack until they were inside and had a full view of the band and Jessica.

The bandstand had been set up in front of the fireplace. And resting on the mantel, where Elizabeth had left it earlier, was the burial pot. She had been afraid to move it very far away from its source. She didn't want the *old ones* to think she was a grave robber.

Elizabeth watched as Scott turned a dial on his electric guitar. Suddenly, the volume doubled. Elizabeth's hands flew to her ears. She'd never heard anything so loud in her life. It was loud enough to wake the dead.

Elizabeth blinked. The volume must have been affecting her eyesight. She could swear that the walls were shaking.

There was a tap on her shoulder. She turned toward Amy, who was pointing to the walls and then pretending to shake.

The walls really are shaking, then, Elizabeth thought fearfully. Her eyes weren't playing tricks on her.

Then, to her horror, she saw that the slight

movement of the walls was causing the burial pot to teeter dangerously near the edge of the mantel.

Elizabeth held her breath, praying for the music to stop before . . .

Crash!

Elizabeth didn't actually hear the sound, but she felt it as the pot hit the floor and broke into several pieces.

Scott and Jessica drew out the last note of the song as if they were competing for who could hold out the longest. Scott gave up first, his voice fading out while Jessica's went on and on.

The crowd went wild as Jessica pumped her fist in the air, but Elizabeth was too numb to appreciate her sister's moment in the spotlight.

As the crowd screamed and applauded, the walls began to shake even more, and there was a low rumbling sound.

"Look out there!" someone near the window cried.

Every head turned toward the window, and Elizabeth had to stand up on tiptoe to see the four skeletons that danced in the moonlight several yards away.

One of the skeletons was headless.

"It's Rick, Bruce, and Jake!" Jessica shouted into the microphone.

"No it's not," a voice yelled from the crowd.

Elizabeth and everybody else gasped as one of the skeletons inside the shack removed his mask.

"Rick!" the crowd gasped.

Then two more skeletons removed their masks. Elizabeth felt her heart pounding. It was Jake and Bruce!

"Then it's Steven and Joe," Janet pronounced. "With a couple of their buddies."

A gorilla and a baboon removed their rubber heads. "None of my buddies," Steven insisted.

"Mine either," Joe said.

Everyone watched as the group of skeletons approached the tree where the skull hung from a nail.

"Great gag!" Bruce Patman roared with laughter.

Elizabeth felt powerless to move, powerless to speak, powerless to do anything except watch in fascinated horror as the headless skeleton reached out, removed the skull, and . . .

"Leave this place!" an eerily loud voice commanded. "Your noise disturbs our rest!"

Elizabeth whirled around. "Kala!"

Kala glared at the crowd with blank, blazing eyes. "Leave this place now!" she commanded, backing out of the door.

The creaking and rumbling of the shack escalated into a roar. There was a loud, tearing sound as one of the interior reinforcement beams ripped away from the wall.

"Everybody get out!" someone yelled. "This place is coming down!"

The cry electrified the crowd. Dozens of people surged toward the door as more of the reinforcement beams came tumbling down around them.

The whole shack began to rattle and shake. Elizabeth felt Amy's hand close over her wrist. "Come on!" Amy urged. "Let's go."

"Where's Jessica?" Elizabeth yelled, trying to twist out of Amy's grasp.

"Jessica is fine. Now *come on*."

Amy yanked Elizabeth's arm and pulled her out the door. A huge crowd of kids surged out behind them, pushing them farther away from the shack just as the entire structure collapsed in a cloud of dust.

"Unbelievable!" Danny Jackson said.

"This is totally freaky," Dennis Cookman moaned.

The crowd milled around the collapsed structure, marveling at what had happened.

"Well," Janet Howell said in a huffy tone. "I guess this is what we get for listening to Mandy!"

"Listening to *me*?" Mandy countered angrily. "I told you we needed more reinforcement on the walls."

"Give it up, Mandy," Janet said haughtily. "Just ask anyone. *I* was always for more reinforcement."

Elizabeth sighed. A headless skeleton could appear at a party and an entire building could collapse, and the Unicorns were their same old selves. She watched as all the Unicorns joined the dispute over whose fault the building's collapse was.

Every Unicorn except Jessica. Elizabeth couldn't help smiling as she watched her sister snuggle deeper into Scott's protective arm.

"Does this mean the party's over?" Ellen Riteman finally whined.

"No way!" Scott said, removing his arm from around Jessica's shoulders. "We got all the instruments out except the drums. The food's safe, out on this ramp. The generator is still working. I say let's just move the party."

"We'll go to my house," Lila announced.

"It's Halloween!" Scott shouted. "Party!"

"Partyyyyy!" everyone shouted as they packed up the food and went to find their bikes.

But Elizabeth was frozen by fear as she remembered the dancing skeleton. She looked over at the tree. The skull was gone. The headless skeleton was complete at last. Maybe now he, or she, would rest.

"So you don't remember *anything* about coming to the party?" Jessica asked for about the fifteenth time. It was after school on Wednesday, and Elizabeth, Jessica, and Kala were standing outside the remains of the shack.

Kala shook her head. "Not a thing. And if anybody but Elizabeth had told me that I'd come and delivered a warning, I would think they were playing some kind of trick on me." She prodded the rubble of the old shack with her shovel. "I don't remember falling asleep or anything. It was like one minute I was in my room, and the next minute I was coming in the front door. My mom was freaked out because she didn't know where I'd been."

"What did you tell her?" Elizabeth asked.

"I just told her I'd stopped by a party," Kala answered. "I didn't even know that was sort of the truth. I'll tell her what really happened soon, though. Jack Whitefeather said he would help me explain."

"Do you really think the shack collapsed because the old ones were angry about the noise?" Jessica asked. "Or do you think it collapsed because we goofed up on the construction?"

Elizabeth shrugged. "I don't know. I guess we'll never know."

"Well, believe it or not, it was the greatest night of my whole life," Jessica said happily. "Scott told me it was the wildest Halloween he'd ever had. And he put his arm around me twice, and all the Unicorns saw it."

Elizabeth smiled. Typical Jessica. She spent an evening with ghosts and skeletons, but what really impressed her was having a high school guy put his arm around her.

Just then she heard a cry of surprise. "Here's a piece," Jack Whitefeather called out triumphantly from the other side of the wreckage.

Elizabeth, Jessica, and Kala hurried over to join Jack and Mr. Fowler.

Jack had returned to town the night before and

called Elizabeth first thing in the morning. When he had heard what she had to say, he'd agreed to call Mr. Fowler himself and talk him into visiting the property. Luckily, he convinced Mr. Fowler to drive back to Sweet Valley right away.

"Here's another one," Kala said, leaning over to retrieve a broken piece of pot.

Jack took the piece from her and held the shards up side by side. They fit together like the pieces of a jigsaw puzzle, and the group could see the whole figure of the bear and a fragment of the bat.

"My gosh." Mr. Fowler gasped. "I've seen pots like that in museums."

"It's a shame this one is broken," Jack said sadly. "But I would be willing to bet that there are others just like it buried all over this place."

Mr. Fowler reached into his pocket and removed one of the stone arrowheads that Elizabeth had shown him. He looked at it thoughtfully. Finally, he glanced at Jack. "So you're convinced this place is a burial ground?"

Jack nodded. "There are a lot of bones in this ground. Old bones that shouldn't be disturbed."

Mr. Fowler squinted out toward the woods. "It's a beautiful spot," he murmured, almost to himself.

The air around them was suddenly heavy with the thudding sound of beating wings.

Every face turned upward, and they all gasped.

"It's an eagle," Mr. Fowler said in a tone of wonder. "I haven't seen one of those in years."

The eagle disappeared over the trees.

"It was incredible!" Elizabeth exclaimed.

"If we don't protect them," Jack Whitefeather said, "they'll be gone forever. And so will the bears and the bats and the wolves."

Mr. Fowler took a few steps toward the woods. Then he looked all about him. "Old bones deserve respect," he said after a few moments. "And so do rare and beautiful living creatures."

"What are you going to do?" Jack Whitefeather asked.

"Well," Mr. Fowler said, thrusting his hands into his pockets and looking appreciatively around him. "I think we're standing on the Sweet Valley Nature Scout Wildlife Preserve. We'll build a proper clubhouse on the other side of the fence line. And we'll teach the kids about the people who are buried here." He shot a look at Kala and lifted an eyebrow. "*If* you think the old ones will approve."

There was a shrill cry and a loud thudding sound in the wind.

The eagle reappeared over their heads and circled twice before disappearing again behind the treetops.

Elizabeth looked at Kala intently.

Kala smiled at the group gathered around her. Her eyes shone brightly. When she spoke, her voice was quiet. "I think that means they do." She smiled at Elizabeth. "And so do I."

SIGN UP FOR THE SWEET VALLEY HIGH® FAN CLUB!

Hey, girls! Get all the gossip on Sweet Valley High's® most popular teenagers when you join our fantastic Fan Club! As a member, you'll get all of this really cool stuff:

- Membership Card with your own personal Fan Club ID number
- A Sweet Valley High® Secret Treasure Box
- Sweet Valley High® Stationery
- Official Fan Club Pencil (for secret note writing!)
- Three Bookmarks
- A "Members Only" Door Hanger
- Two Skeins of J. & P. Coats® Embroidery Floss with flower barrette instruction leaflet
- Two editions of *The Oracle* newsletter
- Plus exclusive Sweet Valley High® product offers, special savings, contests, and much more!

Be the first to find out what Jessica & Elizabeth Wakefield are up to by joining the Sweet Valley High® Fan Club for the one-year membership fee of only $6.25 each for U.S. residents, $8.25 for Canadian residents (U.S. currency). Includes shipping & handling.

Send a check or money order (do not send cash) made payable to "Sweet Valley High® Fan Club" along with this form to:

SWEET VALLEY HIGH® FAN CLUB, BOX 3919-B, SCHAUMBURG, IL 60168-3919

NAME _____
(Please print clearly)

ADDRESS _____

CITY_____ STATE _____ ZIP_____
(Required)

AGE _____ BIRTHDAY_____ /_____ /_____

A BANTAM SKYLARK BOOK

FRANCINE PASCAL'S
SWEET VALLEY
Twins AND FRIENDS®

Join Jessica and Elizabeth for big adventure in exciting

SWEET VALLEY TWINS AND FRIENDS
SUPER EDITIONS

☐ #1: CLASS TRIP   15588-1/$3.50
☐ #2: HOLIDAY MISCHIEF   15641-1/$3.75
☐ #3: THE BIG CAMP SECRET   15707-8/$3.50
☐ #4: THE UNICORNS GO HAWAIIAN   15948-8/$3.75
☐ SWEET VALLEY TWINS SUPER SUMMER FUN BOOK
  by Laurie Pascal Wenk   15816-3/$3.50

Elizabeth shares her favorite summer projects & Jessica gives you
pointers on parties. Plus: fashion tips, space to record your
favorite summer activities, quizzes, puzzles, a summer calendar,
photo album, scrapbook, address book & more!

SWEET VALLEY TWINS AND FRIENDS
CHILLERS

☐ #1: THE CHRISTMAS GHOST   15767-1/$3.50
☐ #2: THE GHOST IN THE GRAVEYARD   15801-5/$3.50
☐ #3: THE CARNIVAL GHOST   15859-7/$3.50
☐ #4: THE GHOST IN THE BELL TOWER   15893-7/$3.50
☐ #5: THE CURSE OF THE RUBY NECKLACE 15949-6/$3.50

SWEET VALLEY TWINS AND FRIENDS
MAGNA EDITION:

☐ #1: THE MAGIC CHRISTMAS   48051-0/$3.75

Bantam Books, Dept. SVT6, 2451 S. Wolf Road, Des Plaines, IL 60018

Please send me the items I have checked above. I am enclosing $_____
(please add $2.50 to cover postage and handling). Send check or money
order, no cash or C.O.D.s please.

Mr/Ms _____

Address _____

City/State _____ Zip _____

SVT6-8/93

Please allow four to six weeks for delivery.
Prices and availability subject to change without notice.